PUFFIN BOOKS

Editor : Kaye Webb

PS 248

THE ROSE ROUND

Woodhall, the old country house where orphaned
Matthew went to spend his holidays with his sister
Caro, seemed to have been built to hold idyllic happiness, but one by one Matt found flaws in the harmony of
this enclosed little world. It was not only the broken
fountain in the Rose Round which needed repairing. It
was the heart of Mrs Ayre, endlessly mourning the death
of her daughter and her favourite son, resenting big
clumsy Theo who remained, and spoiling her wayward
granddaughter Alix until a near tragedy slowly brought
them all to a better sense of values.

These tragically violent feelings were a profound
surprise to Matthew, yet he was able to watch with
gratitude a gradual smoothing down of smouldering
hatred and sorrows, until the house regained its old
peace, and Caro found the happiness she had so richly
earned.

This story with its strong religious undercurrents (the
hero is a devout Catholic) is movingly told. It will give
deep satisfaction to all children who are puzzled by the
needless unhappiness they see in the world.

For older children.

D1342172

CATHERINE

MERIOL TREVOR

THE ROSE ROUND

ILLUSTRATIONS BY PHILIP GOUGH

PENGUIN BOOKS

Penguin Books Ltd, Harmondsworth, Middlesex, England
Penguin Books Pty Ltd, Ringwood, Victoria, Australia

—

First published by Hamish Hamilton 1963
Published in Puffin Books 1966

—

Copyright © Meriol Trevor, 1963

—

Made and printed in Great Britain by
Cox & Wyman Ltd, London, Fakenham and Reading
Set in Monotype Garamond

Contents

1 The House in the Wood   *page* 7
2 The Gate into the Garden   14
3 The Empty Rooms   21
4 The Owner of Woodhall   32
5 Nero Scared   45
6 Bertrand's Tower   54
7 Trouble for Theo   64
8 More Trouble   73
9 Exchange of Blows   84
10 West Wind Blowing   95
11 Dark November   104
12 Dangerous Christmas   114
13 The Fate of a Ring   126
14 Cold North Gate   135
15 Alix Kept Down   147
16 Danger in the Dark Night   159
17 After the Accident   171
18 A Way for Madame   181
19 The Hours are Counted   188
20 East Gate of Spring   198

I

The House in the Wood

THE first time Matt went to Woodhall it was June, it was midsummer and the sun shone all day long in the middle of the blue sky. All the fields were green with corn as he went through them, the meadows with long grass waving till the hay-cutter came, or short and emerald where the cows were grazing, for there had been days of rain, but now the rain was gone, cleared off as if it had never been and all the middle country of England lay bright around as he went through, going in the train.

It was half-term and Matt was going to visit his sister. He had no mother or father, but he had this stepsister who was fifteen years older and always looked after him. Her name was Caroline Rendal, but Matt called her Caro. He was just thirteen. In term time, now, he lived in Birmingham with Aunt Maud Baker, who was elderly and widowed and had never had any children. She thought it was her duty to help 'poor Caroline' with Matthew, as she always called him, so that he came almost to dislike the sound of his whole name. For Aunt Maud thought Matt a clumsy, untidy nuisance of a boy, and told him so several times a day. Luckily he was at school till tea-time most days. But now Birmingham and school and Aunt Maud's tiny tidy brick house were left behind, and Matt was going to visit his sister in the place where she was working.

It was something of a mystery to Matt, this place called Woodhall, because it seemed such a big house, and yet there were not many servants there to run it. Caro was doing the cooking, but she said nobody else lived in except an old French Mademoiselle who did the flowers and dusted the best china ornaments. The housework was done daily by women who came up from the village.

Caro's jobs were usually in schools, so that she could have holidays with Matt, but last term she had got engaged to be married to a man called Jasper Hartnoll. Jasper was tall and handsome and had a Jaguar and a good job in a Birmingham firm, and he did not like Caro working as cook in a school and so she gave it up.

'Just think, Matt,' she said. 'When I'm married we shall have a home of our own and you can have a room just as you like, just exactly as you like.'

But Matt was gloomy. He did not like Jasper Hartnoll. He had a feeling Jasper would spoil any home for him. He also felt Jasper did not like him, thought he was stupid and a nuisance and wished Caro had no relations.

Suddenly one day Caro told Matt she was going to take a job again.

'What will Jasper say?' he asked, very surprised.

'I shan't tell him till I'm there,' said Caro. She then explained that Jasper's father was a very rich man and not only director of his firm but a baronet as well, Sir Godfrey Hartnoll. It turned out that when Jasper had started to tell him he wanted to marry Caro, Sir Godfrey had got very angry indeed and had refused to listen at all. Jasper was his only son and would be Sir Jasper one day and inherit all his money, and Sir Godfrey was furious at the idea of his wanting to marry a girl who was nothing but a cook, because somehow he found out about her job and despised her at once because of it.

'So we have got to wait and get him used to the idea

slowly,' said Caro. 'And I would rather go on earning my own living till it's all settled.'

So she took this job doing the cooking in a big house near Bewdley in the country of the Wyre Forest, beyond Severn. Her letters for the first half of term had been very hurried and Matt only knew that her employer was an old lady called Mrs Ayre, who was French by birth, and was known as 'Madame' and who lived alone in the big house with her granddaughter Alix.

Now, on this hot bright afternoon, Matt arrived in Bewdley, beautiful in its warm red brick against the dark wooded hills, hanging above the great deep sliding Severn, the most mysterious of all the rivers in England.

Caro had come to meet him. There she was, in a white blouse and a bright yellow skirt, with her gold hair coiled in a high knot at the back of her head like a girl of ancient Greece, and her brown eyes smiling at him out of her golden face. Matt thought Caro was beautiful: so did a great many other people. Perhaps if Jasper's father had seen her he would have decided it didn't matter that she had no money and had worked as a cook in schools for most of her life since she grew up, and her father died. Mr Rendal had been a schoolmaster; Matt could just remember him, tall and grey-haired, a man whose frequent chuckles often turned into fits of coughing.

Caro and Matt had tea together in Bewdley and then they lugged Matt's case to a bus and went hurtling away along narrow country roads. They got out of the bus outside some great gates, miles from anywhere it seemed to Matt. Tall trees stood up all round. Leaves hung in green murmuring clouds high over their heads. They were in the forest country. The posts of the gates were lichened, the brick and stone crumbling. On top of each post was a stone eagle with wings half-spread and beak raised.

'The eagle is the Ayre family crest,' said Caro, as they went through the little gate beside the big ones. The iron was rusty on all of them, the paint flaking off in big bubbles and blisters. Grass was growing in places along the middle of the gravel drive.

'No money left,' said Caro.

'But no one could live here without any money,' said Matt.

'It would be a lot to us,' Caro agreed. 'But not enough to keep up a great place like this. Most of the garden has gone wild.'

Matt stared up the straight drive. Each side tall lime trees stood, lacing overhead their smooth shadows of leaves. Far away at the end of the avenue he saw the front of a house, looking small because it was so remote, red brick with long rows of windows.

'I thought only Dukes and people lived in places like this,' Matt said. 'They're not Dukes, are they? She's not even Lady Somebody.'

'No,' said Caro. 'But they are an old family.'

'Everybody's family must be *old*,' Matt pointed out. He was rather given to pedantic considerations of this kind.

Caro laughed. 'Well, long established in the ruling class, then,' she said. 'They were probably fighting in the Wars of the Roses for all I know. As for Madame, it's a continual surprise to me that her family survived the French Revolution. She still behaves as if it had not happened.'

'Don't you like her?'

Caro made a face. 'She is very particular. And listen, Matt, she says on no account are you to go into their part of the house, or the garden.'

'Why on earth not?'

'She's a queer old creature. She says she hates men. She doesn't really, of course. But she is very fussy and thinks a boy about the place would upset everything. She nearly did not engage me when she heard about you, but I think she finds it hard to get a cook who will stay here, so far from the town and so lonely. Anyway, she doesn't want her precious little Alix contaminated by a rough boy. I dare say she's afraid Alix would get rough herself for she has plenty of spirit, that child, from what I've seen of her. Too much, even.'

'How old is she?'

'Thirteen, like you.'

'Well, I don't want to meet her particularly,' said Matt, but he was offended all the same at not being considered fit to associate with the child of this ancient house.

Caro took him down a side walk through trees and more trees and shrubberies, so that they came out at the side of the house instead of at the front. Front and back were both grand and formal, but here at the side was a small rambling town of utilitarian buildings, a big paved yard and long stables with a clock tower. The hands of the clock stood at twelve.

'Stopped,' said Matt, squinting up in the sun. It was warm here, now that they were out of the shade of the trees.

'It stopped years ago,' said Caro.

They were both very tired of lugging Matt's case by now, and put it down with a crash inside the back door. The kitchens and sculleries were enormous regions, but there was no one in them, only a tabby cat asleep in the old basket-chair near the shining black kitchen range.

Caro took Matt up the uncarpeted back stairs, two

flights of them, to his high room, small and bare, looking out on the stable yard.

'Mine's here,' she said, showing him. 'The bathroom's on the floor below, built over the old wash-house.'

Caro had made her room look like herself by filling it with flowers and pinning up her favourite postcards from the National Gallery. On the window-sill stood her little porcelain Madonna and Child which came from Italy, and a big curled shell which she had found on the Norfolk sands last summer. Matt picked it up at once and held it to his ear and immediately he heard the long slow breathing of the sea, the soft roar, the echoing sigh of the waters that flow all round England, washing up and down our shores always till the end of the world.

'How strange to listen to the sea here in the very middle of England,' he said. 'There's no sea here, not for miles. It's all ground.'

He put the shell down again and heard instead a soft croodling and cooing outside. From the window he could see two white birds sidling and pecking in the yard.

'Doves,' said Caro. 'Pigeons, really. Price gave them to me.'

'Who's Price?'

'He's an old man who lives in a cottage by the other gate of the park,' said Caro. 'He does all the odd jobs about the place, the last of all the servants who used to live here when Madame first came, before the First World War.'

'What a long time ago!' Matt said, looking down at the empty yard, and the clock that had stopped one long-ago noon, or had it stopped at midnight?

'I must start getting the dinner now,' said Caro.

'Do they have dinner in the evening?'

'Do they not!' said Caro. 'Madame eats very little, but she has to have all the courses presented just the same. It's good for my cooking after so many boys' meals!'

'Does Alix have dinner?'

'Yes, she does now that she's thirteen.'

But Matt did not see either Madame or Alix. Instead he met Agnes Orchard, who came up from the village every day to wait at table and do parlour-maid's jobs. She had once lived in the house, Caro told Matt, but now her mother was old and she went back to her cottage every night and bicycled up every morning in time to take Madame's breakfast to her on a tray. Agnes was a heavy, creaky woman with a sallow face and sharp eyes. She knew everything about everyone at Woodhall and in the village too, and was full of gossip about all that went on, not that anything ever seemed to happen in the big house.

After they had washed up the supper things Matt went up with Caro to her room and talked, while the golden light lengthened outside, and slowly, slowly, the sun descended from his great height and darkness began to slide up out of the woods.

And when he lay at last in his small hard bed Matt thought how still it was, how very still. The house was full of silence, like a dark pond, the woods outside were still, unstirred by wind, the sky stood up above with all its lacepoint of stars, soundless as a dream. And when he heard, out of the night of trees, an owl hoot, far off, it only made the silence seem more intense when it closed in again.

2

The Gate into the Garden

THE next day was Saturday and Caro was very busy cooking, making puddings and cakes for Sunday. Matt explored all the outbuildings and the stables, and discovered that three of the boxes were in use, though the horses were not at home. Caro said they were probably in the paddock, or perhaps Price was exercising them. Matt wondered if he would have a chance to learn to ride here, an old ambition of his, but thought it was not probable, if Madame was so hostile to boys.

In the afternoon he and Caro went into a meadow behind the house and lay on a rug, talking and reading, but not for long, because Caro had to go and get tea for the family. They saw Agnes bicycling sedately up the drive. She sometimes went back to the village in the afternoon, and sometimes did not.

After Matt had had his tea he wandered out alone into the woods beyond the meadow. The sun was still high, but the light was beginning to take on the tone of evening, slanting through the trees, piercing through their heavy loads of leaves. Matt wandered along little paths, not really going anywhere, idling and dreaming. He wondered if there had been outlaws here, once long ago, like Robin Hood in Sherwood Forest. This was an old forest too, always growing here since trees began to grow in England, long before there were any houses, even the Ayres' house, centuries old, before there were any people even. He stood still, gazing at an ivy-grown oak, longest lived of trees, and thought how secret it was, going on growing there year after year while people in the house were born and lived and died, and went away and came home, and the tree knew none of it, but just went on growing in its green silence. It was not exactly frightening, and yet it made his skin shiver a little, standing here alone among so many trees, all living, but none aware of living. It was like diving under the surface of the sea: all is other and unknown in that deep pond of shade.

Turning away from the tree he saw a decrepit wall, all grown over with ivy and plants, but tall, seven foot tall at least, and still strong enough to stand. In the wall was a very old door, that had once been painted blue, but now the faded paint had peeled and scaled away almost to the wood. There was a keyhole in the door.

Immediately he saw it Matt wanted to look through the keyhole.

He went up to the door and put his hands against it as he bent down to look, and it gave a little under his hands.

Through the hole he saw, bright and small, a blaze of colours, flowers growing. Then the door creaked and leant inwards, rather than opened. The lock was out, but the metal had all rusted away, and Matt's weight had broken it through. He stood up and took hold of the door and lifted it on its complaining hinges and shifted it ajar. Then he squeezed through sideways and there he was on the other side of the wall.

He stood on an overgrown path in the middle of flowers, flowers growing anyhow, crowding each other out, and full of bees. It was very still in the walled garden, and very hot, heavy with sweet and aromatic scents. The path he was on was lined with box hedges that needed trimming. The warm smell of the box was very strong. Matt pushed along the path towards a high yew hedge which shut out his view. There was a gap where the path ran and when he reached that he stopped dead, with a gasp of surprise.

The yew hedge, taller than a man, ran round in a wide circle, enclosing a lawn of mown grass. In the centre of the lawn was a rose garden, and the garden was made like a ring. A high trellis of iron and wire ran all round, rising into arches at the four points of the compass. Matt had come in from the south, and facing him was an arch covered with red roses, high arcs and festoons and garlands of red roses, and through this red rose gate he could see the white ones over the northern arch, and to the west there were yellow, to the east blush roses, all in great profusion, at the peak of bloom.

Inside the trellis ring were beds of bush and standard roses, divided by stone-paved paths, and in the very middle was a fountain of water springing up like a shower of diamonds.

Matt, gazing, spellbound, went slowly closer, went up to the arch of red roses and stepped through it, and was inside the flowering circle. And now he saw two things, almost at once. One was that the fountain was broken in the middle, a jagged stone sticking up there, and the other was that he was not alone in the garden.

A girl was standing behind the broken fountain with the white roses behind her and the sun shining down towards her and away from him, so that his shadow lay before him. She wore a plain white dress and her very black hair was parted in the middle and brushed behind a band of emerald velvet, falling thick to her shoulders. Her face was thin and pointed, her eyebrows sprang apart like antennae: just for a moment Matt thought she was not a real person.

But then she said in a very real and rather suspicious voice, 'What are you doing here?'

'I don't know,' Matt said, confused and dazed. He immediately felt an intruder, clumsy, out of place.

'You must be the cook's brother,' said the girl, looking at him coolly. She had green eyes, like a cat.

Matt flushed. It somehow sounded insulting to call Caro the cook, though that was what she always called herself.

'Is this part of the garden?' he said. 'Of Woodhall, I mean.'

'Of course it is,' said the girl. 'I'm Alix Ayre and I live here. What's your name?'

'Matt,' he said, 'Matthew Rendal.'

'How peculiar,' said Alix. 'I've never met anyone called Matthew.'

'I've never met anyone called Alix,' said Matt. 'Not a girl.'

'It's an old French name,' said Alix proudly. 'Like Alice, really.' She came round the fountain.

'Your sister's much too beautiful to be a cook,' she said. 'You aren't a bit like her.'

Matt knew this well enough. He was large and awkward and bony, instead of plump and neat like Caro. He had rough brown hair and grey eyes and a sticking-out chin.

'I'm just ordinary,' he said.

'I thought you'd talk Cockney,' said Alix. 'Like poor children in books.'

'That's a rude remark,' said Matt. 'Even if I didn't talk like you, you shouldn't say so.'

'I wouldn't, if you didn't,' said Alix, unabashed, but not very coherent. 'Where do you go to school?'

'In Birmingham,' said Matt.

'How peculiar,' said Alix, still coolly staring.

'I think you're awful,' said Matt, with sudden irritation. But Alix laughed.

'Now that's a much ruder remark!' she said. 'And just as I was thinking it was lucky you had found the old gate and come in.'

Matt immediately felt less hostile.

'Well, if you feel like that,' he said, 'why not ask your grandmother if I can't come through the front way?'

'Oh no,' said Alix. 'You don't know Gran'mère. She's quite different from anybody else. Besides, she thinks I might catch something from you.'

'What?' Matt asked suspiciously.

'Not fleas, stupid,' said Alix. 'Not even bad language, but some illness. She thinks Rosario caught her illness from the gardener's boy whom she played with.'

'Who's Rosario?'

'She was Gran'mère's daughter, her first child,' said Alix solemnly, evidently reciting a history as well known to her as her own life. 'She was born in nineteen-twelve and she was very pretty and gay and she only lived to be seven. She died of the influenza after the First World War. Gran'mère was so very unhappy, she has never been the same woman since, she has told me that herself. Mademoiselle says she lives in the past.'

'Didn't she have any other children then?' Matt asked.

'Oh yes, she had two sons after the war. Her husband, my grandfather, was a soldier, you understand.' Matt noticed the old-fashioned way she talked, a little like a girl in a Victorian book. 'I am the daughter of the younger

18

son, Julian,' said Alix seriously. 'He was her favourite, after Rosario, and he was killed at the end of the Second World War, about when I was born. After that, she shut the gates. That's what Mademoiselle says: she shut the gates and returned in her mind to the past. She does not care what happens in the world. I am all she cares for now.'

Matt looked at her. She seemed unconscious of her oddity.

'Don't you go to school?' he said suddenly.

'No. Mademoiselle teaches me. Also Mr Howell comes to give me music lessons,' said Alix.

'But you have some friends?'

'No,' said Alix. 'That's why I am glad you came. It's fun to talk to someone who isn't old, even if it is only a boy.'

'What do you mean, only a boy?' said Matt, feeling insulted again.

'Boys are stupid creatures,' said Alix. 'They only like fighting and football, Gran'mère says so.'

'How does she know, if she doesn't know any boys?' said Matt, with a snort. 'I like lots of things.'

'What sort of things?'

'Well, swimming, and drawing and reading and going to the theatre and collecting matchboxes,' said Matt at random.

'Matchboxes!' cried Alix, but before she could say any more they heard a high old voice calling, 'Alix! Alix! Where are you?'

'It's Gran'mère!' Alix said. 'Quick, out of the gate at once!'

'But why?' Matt objected.

She caught his shoulder and turned him round, pushing him away.

19

'Go on, go!' she said. 'We shall meet again. It's a secret. Gran'mère would not understand. She would be angry. Go on, Matthew, please.'

Matt went. He ran through the gap in the yew hedge, and along the box-bordered path through the flowery wilderness; he squeezed through the old blue door sideways and was suddenly in the green cool space of the woods again, under the heavy summer murmuring of the leaves.

He did not tell Caro he had been in the rose garden and met Alix.

3

The Empty Rooms

THE next day was Sunday, and after breakfast a big ancient Rolls Royce was taken out of the garage in the yard, which was the old coach-house. It was Price who took the car out. Price was grey-haired and old and silent and he wore a uniform with a navy-blue peaked cap and long black polished boots. The car was to take them to mass. They got in and drove round to the front door.

Now Matt expected to see old Mrs Ayre, but he did not. Only Alix came out, in her Sunday coat and hat, and she sat in the back with Caro. Matt sat in front with Price, who said not a word. Nor did Alix. She sat very upright and looked past Matt as if she had never seen him before, and hardly noticed him now.

Matt was disconcerted. He had a sudden strange feeling that his going into the rose garden was a dream. The harder he tried to convince himself that it had happened, the more doubtful he became.

But as they got out of the car on their return Alix suddenly pushed something into his hand, quickly and secretly, and went into the house, still without really looking at him. Matt went up to his room and opened the tiny folded square of paper. On it was written in a firm black script: 'My grandmother is going out to tea. Meet me at four in the Rose Round. Alix. PS. Bring your tea. Don't tell your sister.'

Matt was a little doubtful of not telling Caro, but after all she would only say no and he wanted to go. So he asked to take his tea in the woods and she let him, giving him sandwiches and cake and lemonade in a knapsack. Matt had a watch, but it seemed a very long time after lunch till four o'clock. At five minutes to four he went through the old blue door and peered cautiously round the gap in the yew hedge. Alix was just coming through the gap on the other side, carrying a basket. She waved to him and they met on the grass.

Alix would not spend much time over tea. 'I want to show you things indoors,' she said. 'Before Gran'mère comes home.'

'But won't somebody see us?'

'No. Mademoiselle always spends Sunday afternoon in her room, till dinner-time, and today she'll have the blinds down because she has a headache. That's why she didn't come to mass. It was lucky, because it would have been difficult to give you the note with her watching me.'

Matt was keen enough to see the house and ate up his sandwiches with a will. They left basket and knapsack on the lawn and went through the rose garden towards the house. As they passed the fountain Matt noticed again that it was broken. There had once been some decorative piece in the centre: now all that remained was the jagged base of it. He paused by the sparkling brim, standing still in the hot sun.

'When is it going to be mended?'

'Never,' said Alix, looking at him.

'Never?'

She shook her head. 'The rose garden has been here a long time, but Gran'mère had the fountain made when Rosario was born, and there was a statue in the middle, of Our Lady I think, and when Rosario died she had it taken away. Price told me.'

'He can talk then,' Matt observed.

'I made him,' said Alix. 'He doesn't like to, I admit. But he'll always talk about Grandfather, who was his captain or something in the First World War, and you can get round to other things like that.'

'Rosario is a queer name,' said Matt.

'Not abroad,' said Alix. 'She was born on the feast of Our Lady of the Rosary, in October. Mary Rosario, she was. I'll show you a picture of her.'

They came out beside the house, the long red brick garden front of it, silent, serene, in the hot midsummer light. Alix took Matt in by a glass-panelled door. He paused on the threshold, looking back. The woods were all round Woodhall, but the old house stood on a slight rise in the middle of a wide saucer-like dip in the hills, and the trees had been cut, long centuries ago, to make vistas in three directions, spreading out like the spokes of a fan. They ran like wide green roads through the dark trees up to the brow of the ridge. At the end of the one in the centre was a white-pillared summer-house like a little temple with a dome and a squat tower behind it, and in the others there were statues. The green grass, the dark trees, the blue sky and the white statues made Matt feel more than ever that he had walked into a dream.

He went into the house, which was very still. Slatted blinds were drawn down over the south and west windows, thin bars of light lay across the old carpets, on the polished floors. Alix went on ahead, light-footed, careless, confident, at home. Matt followed her, anxious, uncertain, curious, the intruder.

They seemed to him to go through so many rooms, all empty, all full of stiff old furniture, of dark oil-paintings, of ornaments and embroideries. There was no time to look at them properly; Alix kept hurrying him on, flitting ahead through the warm, dim air. Now she took him upstairs and along passages and at last into a little room with windows on three sides, and the windows were all barred. It was a nursery. There was a rocking-horse, yellowed with age, a dolls' house full of small dusty furniture, and dolls with china faces sitting in a disconsolate row with their backs to the wall.

'It's her nursery,' Alix said. 'There she is.'

Matt saw a picture hanging above the fireplace. There was the little girl whose sudden death had so affected her mother, who had come from a French château so long ago to marry an Englishman.

In a way it was a relief to see Rosario's picture. She was so gay and laughing, swinging her sun-bonnet in her hand, standing all among leaves and roses, her cheeks red, her brown eyes bright as a bird's, her hair all a dark curly tangle round her cheerful face.

'Rosario,' said Matt slowly, and he smiled.

Alix was watching him. 'She always makes me smile too,' she said. 'But Gran'mère, it makes her sad. She won't come in here. She says she has never forgiven God for taking her away. She won't go to mass any more.'

'She lets you go.'

'Oh yes, because she says it is the proper thing for a young girl,' said Alix.

Matt was silent, not knowing what to say to that. But presently he asked, 'Was it Rosario's picture you wanted to show me?'

'Oh no, not particularly,' said Alix. 'It was some of my own things. Come along.'

They left the empty nursery and went along a passage.

'What a big house this is,' Matt said. 'Don't you get lost in it?'

'I know it too well,' said Alix.

She took him into a room where the windows, un-blinded, faced the sun which streamed in across the polished boards.

'My room,' Alix said.

The first thing Matt saw was a great harp standing up, a curved triangle of gold, with the sunbeams slanting through its taut strings.

'A harp!' he cried. 'Can you play a harp?'

'Mr Howell teaches me,' said Alix. She went to the harp and carefully played two chords and an arpeggio. The resonant boom of the strings echoed in the air.

'I mustn't rouse old Mademoiselle,' said Alix. 'Look, what do you think of this?'

She took something out of a corner and the next minute was flashing a sword in his face. Matt jumped backwards and Alix laughed.

'It's Grandfather's sword,' she said.

'Let me see.'

She let him hold the sword in his hand, but not for long.

'What else can I show you?' she said, skipping rest-lessly about.

Matt saw a miniature by the fireplace. 'Who's this?' he asked, looking at a boy's face, thin, blue-eyed, crowned with fair hair.

'That's Julian, my father, when he was young,' said Alix.

'You're not a bit like him.'

'Gran'mère says the bones of my face are. Now what shall we do?'

Matt, who had expected to be shown something in-teresting, was disappointed.

'Perhaps I had better go away now,' he said, looking at his watch.

'But you've only just come,' said Alix, dismayed.

'Suppose your grandmother came back? Let's go back in the garden.' The house, with its crowded empty rooms, suddenly oppressed him.

'Yes, all right.' Alix was evidently pleased that he was not going away altogether.

But just as they were going down the wide shallow stairs the front door opened and a small upright old lady came into the hall.

'Gran'mère!' whispered Alix, alarmed.

There was no excape. She looked up at once and saw them.

'Alix! Who is that boy?'

'It's Matthew, Gran'mère. Miss Rendal's brother.'

'I told her he was not to be allowed in the house,' said Madame. She spoke English with precision and only a trace of a French accent.

'Caro didn't know,' said Matt. 'I met Alix in the garden.'

'Come down here,' said Madame, tapping the floor with her silver-headed black cane.

They went down together and came face to face with her. She had very bright brown eyes, like Rosario, Matt suddenly thought, but these were somehow hard and cold, like beads. She scrutinized Matt for a moment and then said, 'I do not like this boy. He reminds me of Théodore.' She pronounced this name 'Téodore'. Matt had no idea who 'Théodore' was, but it was evident that he was someone Madame did not like. She turned suddenly to a tall grey-haired man who had come in behind her. 'Does he not remind you of Théodore at that age, Godfrey?'

. . . came face to face with her.

'A little, perhaps,' said he. 'He's big and awkward like Theo.' He pronounced the 'h' in the name in the English way.

'Except that this one is not so ugly and does not seem to have anything wrong with him,' said the old lady. 'It proves what I have always said, that Théodore is a throwback to some bad blood in the family.' She turned on Matt again. 'Go back to the kitchen, boy. I do not wish to see you here again.'

Matt was so furious he felt he was going to choke. He knew he had gone red in the face. He wished he could be cool and say something very crushing, but he could not speak at all.

'Well, I like Matthew myself,' said Alix. 'It's dreadfully dull only to speak to old people all the time. I must say, sometimes I feel like running away.'

'Don't be ridiculous, child,' said Madame, with an irritated snort.

'It isn't ridiculous!' cried Alix. 'Sometimes I think it's like being shut up in a museum here. I don't see why I have got to live alone, without friends, always and always!'

She turned and fled up the stairs and away along the silent passages.

Madame clicked her tongue. 'What a drama!' she said, dryly. 'I shall have a time when she is a few years older. If your Jasper will only wait, Godfrey, she would make him a pretty wife, and that would settle them both.'

'Jasper is already trying to marry some penniless domestic servant he's picked up in Birmingham,' said the grey-haired man. 'Never heard such nonsense in my life.'

Matt forgot his own predicament in the horrified

realization that this must be Sir Godfrey Hartnoll, Jasper's rich father. What would Caro say if she knew he was a friend of her employer's? He must live near too, if, as he guessed, Madame had been to tea with him.

'Jasper won't be such a fool as to throw away his future for a little servant,' said Madame. 'If he were to marry Alix in about five years' time, they could live here.'

'And what about Theodore?'

'It matters not at all about him,' said Madame. 'He will not oppose me. He would not dare.' She turned round and saw Matt standing there with his mouth open.

'Have you not gone yet, great fool of a boy?' she said sharply. 'Go at once. At once!'

Matt did not know which way to go. He made for the nearest door and rushed through it. It banged shut behind him, on a spring.

He was in a long gallery lined with books, with a black and white paved floor and busts of famous men ranged along the top of the bookcases. There was Plato and Cicero and Virgil and Dante and Alexander Pope and Goethe and Voltaire and Lord Macaulay, and they all somehow looked rather alike in their white plaster. The rows of leather-bound books looked as if no one ever read them. But in one of the alcoves there was a book left open on a table, and someone's notebook and pencil beside it. Suddenly curious, Matt went and had a look.

The book was written in funny English with extra unknown letters, and looked a little like German. In the notebook someone had evidently been trying to put it into modern English verse. It seemed to be a poem about the Phoenix, but the versions were so mixed up and crossed out that it was hard to read.

Then Matt remembered Madame's dismissal and hurried on through the library and out into a kind of pillared hall and on through another door and then he was brought up short and gasped in surprise.

For he was in a chapel; long windows ranged each side, the western light slanting in sideways on the faded blue carpet. Above the altar hung a tapestry and against it a big crucifix; there were candles on the altar, but yellow with age and lack of use, and it was covered with a blue cloth. It was very still in there and airless. All the windows were shut and it felt as if no one ever went there.

Matt stared round the chapel in silence. It was empty, like all the other rooms in the house, it was old, unused, musty like them. Yet he felt suddenly and strongly that he ought to say a prayer here. So he knelt down on the blue carpet, and then, remembering Rosario, he asked for her to rest in peace and in perpetual light.

'And why does her mother mind so much, if she is living in perpetual light?' he thought, and got up and went out of the chapel, shutting the door on its dusty silence.

In the pillared ante-chapel was a door into the garden, and in the end he got back to the kitchen and to Caro that way, and told her everything that had happened.

'Sir Godfrey Hartnoll living near here!' she said. 'Oh dear, now I have made a mess of things! Jasper will be furious.'

'I thought his father was beastly,' said Matt.

Caro laughed. 'I'm sure he isn't!' she said.

'I mean, he was so very high and mighty,' said Matt. 'And Madame was rude, and they both called you a servant.'

'Well, so I am. Not a bad thing to be, either.'

'Yes, but the way they said it!'

'Matt, love, it's not worth worrying over,' said Caro. 'But I'm sorry for poor little Alix shut up in this place. No wonder she's rather odd.'

Matt sighed, thinking of the house. 'It's so beautiful,' he said. 'And it's so dead.'

4

The Owner of Woodhall

NOTHING very much happened on Monday, the last day
of Matt's holiday. In the morning he went into the stables
and found Price grooming a very big black horse. Price
gave him a slight nod and after several minutes of watching him Matt said, 'What a big horse that is.'

Price straightened his back, pausing.

'Has to carry a big man,' he said.

'A man?' said Matt, surprised, for Woodhall seemed
inhabited only by women. 'Who, please?'

'Mr Ayre,' said Price.

'I thought they were all dead,' said Matt.

'Mr Theodore Ayre is the owner of Woodhall,' Price
said, and went on with his work.

'I thought Madame owned it,' said Matt.

'No.'

It was very difficult to talk to Price. Matt made one
more effort. 'What relation is he to Madame, then?'

'Her son,' said Price.

He said no more, and Matt gave it up and went away,
back to the house. Caro knew nothing about Mr Ayre
except that he existed, and Agnes Orchard had gone back
home to see how her mother was getting on, so Matt's
curiosity was left unsatisfied.

In the evening he had to go back to Birmingham.

'See you at the end of July,' said Caro, kissing him
good-bye. 'We will have some fun then, on my days
off.'

The sun still shone, hot and still, over Woodhall as Matt went away.

Birmingham seemed enormous, clanging, smoke-darkened, after that silent green place. Aunt Maud welcomed him back with a grumble.

'You should have come back on an earlier train. Now I suppose you are hungry as usual, and I've had my supper.'

'May I make some for myself?' Matt asked.

Aunt Maud allowed this. Matt fried bacon and eggs on the gas stove in the tiny kitchen, and after he had eaten and washed up, he went to say good night to his aunt. She was reading a local paper.

'Is this one of your Ayre family, do you think?' she asked, and read out. '"Mr Ayre told our reporter that the closing of the school would be a tragedy and he and Mr Kingston hoped to take the children elsewhere."'

'I shouldn't think so,' said Matt. 'They're much too grand to be mixed up with schools. Alix doesn't even go to one.'

He went upstairs to his little room and slowly went to bed. He could not get Woodhall out of his mind. The rows of houses under the smoky darkening sky, the hoots and bumpings of trains, cars rushing by in the streets not far off, all these seemed less real than the empty house in the middle of the trees, and the ring of roses where he had met Alix.

He was not asleep, and yet not altogether awake, vividly aware of that round garden, as if he were standing in the archway with the red roses over his head, and looking out, southward. South: over the green fields and small towns of southern England, over the emerald ditch of the channel, over great sun-baked France, down to the blue pond of the Mediterranean. And then what? Africa, the great desert, the miles of waste land, gaunt, waterless, where only wanderers lived. And then, farther, that other Africa of mountain and deep forest, the jungles where wild beasts roamed, the haunt of ancient magic, unknown rites, hidden people: a place of danger and mystery. Farther south still his inward eye travelled on and came to the cold continent of ice, Antarctica, where the pole of the world was, and blizzards ruled, and long night, and lifeless snow, the beautiful and terrible dead land, like the moon.

Then he turned round in his mind and looked through the rose gate inward, and saw, suddenly, a golden lion sitting, heraldic, on the step of the fountain.

Perhaps after all he was asleep then, perhaps that was a dream.

Woodhall itself began to seem a dream as he went to and from school every day on the bus, and learned his lessons, and swapped matchboxes with his friend Tunstall, and played cricket, rather successfully, for he had a good eye, and ragged with the others and fought sometimes, and bought ice-cream with the pocket money he always meant to save and never could, and went to the cinema, especially if there was a western or a space story on, and grew and grew every day, Aunt Maud said, grumbling because his clothes split and he ate so much.

But when term came to an end, everything seemed suddenly dull and dusty and grey in Birmingham, and Tunstall went off to Wales with his parents and there was nothing interesting to do any more, so then Matt remembered Woodhall as a place and not a dream, and was glad it was in the country. In spite of Madame's prohibitions he would have all the woods and the fields to wander in. So off he went in the train again and Aunt Maud said she was glad to see the back of him.

It was not settled weather as it had been in June, but changeable and thundery. Great clouds banked like mountains westward, dark over the dark woods, leaning threateningly above Bewdley as he arrived. Price had come to fetch him this time, not in the Rolls but in an old rattling shooting-brake he used to do errands for Madame.

He nodded to Matt, but never said a word the whole way.

Caro had not come. She met Matt in the doorway and kissed him.

'Darling, I'm in a terrible rush. Sir Godfrey is coming to dinner, and Lady Hartnoll too, and their eldest daughter. Thank goodness Agnes Orchard does the waiting at table, so they won't see me. Jasper has found out where I am and he's horrified. He keeps writing to tell me to leave at once, but after all, Madame pays well and I can't ask Jasper to keep us till we're married.'

Matt found himself swept up in the dinner preparations. He peeled almonds for Caro, and ate several. He polished up glasses and silver and put the things through the hatch for Agnes when she laid the table. As usual she was full of gossip and comments on the two families.

'Lady Hartnoll was old Mr Ayre's sister,' she said. 'But she and Madame don't hit it off very well, never did. Lady Hartnoll's frightened of her, if you ask me. She's always been timid like, lets that daughter of hers rule the roost at home and can't say boo to Sir Godfrey.'

Matt thought it would be hard for anyone to say boo to Sir Godfrey. He asked Agnes, 'Did you know Alix's grandfather, Madame's husband?'

'Oh yes,' said Agnes. 'A nice quiet gentleman he was, like all the real military, kind as anything. Mr Julian was like him in looks, but not in himself, if you know what I mean. Spoiled, he was, Madame spoiled him, encouraged all his little fads and tempers, always setting him above his brother.'

'When did old Mr Ayre die?' Matt asked.

'He never lived to be old,' Agnes said. 'He had some of that nasty gas in the first war and he died when his sons were only little boys. A pity, I say, because she wasn't the one to bring up boys. Not that he had any say, the father, I mean. She always got her way with him, like she gets it with everyone. Sir Godfrey is the only man that can manage her, and the only man she admires, to my belief.'

'Is he?' said Matt.

'Ah, she likes a hard man, and he's hard,' said Agnes. 'Always cool and very polite, he is, but he's got an eye for the main chance, all the same. That's why he's a rich man now and Mr Ayre, that died, he never was. Nor this one won't be either, Mr Theo. He's a born fool, if ever there was one. If you ask me, when Madame goes this place will be sold up, and what they get will hardly pay the debts. Go and ask Sis what she's done with the salad servers, there's a good boy.'

'Salad!' said Caro, when Matt told her. 'Oh, that reminds me, Matt, do be a darling and fetch me a garlic.'

'Where from?'

'Out in the yard, third door along. It's a little shed where the gardener hangs onions and things.'

Matt went out into the yard, which was cool and quiet in the gathering dusk after the heat and bustle of the kitchen. He counted the doors. The third one was open so he went straight in, right into someone who was kneeling on the floor with his back to the door. Matt fell over his legs and crashed into his back, which hardly seemed to shake the man at all, but caused Matt to fall sideways to the floor, where he lay, quite dazed with surprise.

The man jumped up, knocked his head on a beam, swore mildly and then bent over Matt.

'Where did you come from?' he said, surprised.

'I'm awfully sorry,' said Matt, sitting up. 'I didn't see you at all.'

It was dark in the shed, and he could not see the man very well now, except to see that he was very big.

'I was looking for something I dropped,' said this man.

'What sort of thing?' Matt asked.

'Well, a key as a matter of fact.'

Matt got on hands and knees and peered round. So did the man he had fallen over.

'There it is,' said Matt, seeing something shining dully in the gloom. He picked it up and handed it over. The big man took it with his left hand, the other seemed to be in a sling.

'Thank you,' he said. 'Now what were you looking for?'

'Garlic,' said Matt.

'Garlic?' said the man, surprised. 'What on earth for?'

'My sister's making a salad,' said Matt. 'She's doing the cooking here. Her name's Caroline Rendal.'

'I haven't met Miss Rendal yet, because I've only just come,' said the man. 'What's your own name?'

'Matt. Matthew.'

'A very good name to have,' said the man. 'Mine is Theo.'

'Oh,' said Matt. 'Are you Mr Theodore Ayre?'

'Yes.'

'Oh,' said Matt again, not quite sure what to do next. 'So that big horse is yours, that black one.'

'Nero? Yes, he is.'

Caro's voice called out for Matt.

'She wants the garlic,' Matt said.

'She has a nice voice,' said Mr Ayre, kneeling on the floor, listening.

Matt saw the garlics on a shelf and took one.

'I'd better go,' he said.

'We shall meet again,' said Mr Ayre, nodding.

Matt went back to the kitchen.

'I met Mr Ayre in there,' he said.

'What nonsense!' said Caro. 'As if he'd be in the shed!'

'Well, he was.'

But Caro was too busy to attend to him.

Matt looked out of a window to see the Hartnolls arrive. They drove up in a great big car, much newer than Madame's. Lady Hartnoll was pale and thin and faded, and wore a dress of beige lace which made her look even paler than she was. Her daughter Freda was quite different. She was tall and determined and Matt thought she looked pretty tough, too. Her brown shoulders rippled with muscle as her fur stole slipped back. She looked as if she would be much more at home in tweeds and brogues than in the green taffeta evening dress she was wearing.

'Jasper's big sister,' Matt told himself, giggling. Jasper had three sisters older than himself and said he hated them all. Two were married, but this one, the eldest, who must be only a couple of years off forty, was not.

Matt helped Agnes by carrying the plates from the kitchen to the hatch and the dirty ones to the pantry. So he was able to look through and see the dinner-party going on. He had to admit that Madame looked impressive in her black long-sleeved, high-necked gown, with a diamond clasp at the throat. Her white hair was done up in a soft pouf on top of her head and she wore many rings on her small blue-veined old hands. She gave most of her attention to Sir Godfrey, who was looking very handsome and distinguished, with his brown beaky face and silvery hair. Matt wondered what he would say if he knew his son's fiancée had cooked the dinner he was eating with relish.

'He ought to be pleased,' Matt thought.

He could just see Mr Ayre, who was sitting at the side of the table, and now that he saw him in the light Matt, who had liked his voice, was disappointed. He was so very large that in evening dress he looked like a coal-heaver who has just been elected to Parliament. Nothing seemed to fit, it was either too loose or too tight, and he looked extremely uncomfortable. He had a wide square sort of face without much pattern in it; it even seemed a bit lopsided to Matt, squinting through the hatch, as if the two sides didn't quite fit together. His eyebrows were very black and thick, and his dark hair grew up thick too, in short tufts like a marshy field. His right arm was in a sling, hidden underneath his coat, which, although it was pinned with a large safety-pin, kept slipping. He was having difficulty in eating with only one hand, sticking desperately to potato because it was easy.

Madame suddenly said in a cold dry voice, 'Send Mr Ayre's food out to be cut up for him, Agnes. He seems incapable of feeding himself.'

Theodore Ayre turned dark red and stared fixedly down at the table.

Agnes brought his plate to the hatch.

'I'll cut it,' whispered Matt, feeling sorry for Mr Ayre, told off like that in front of the visitors. After all, if he had broken his arm, how could he help it? Matt cut up the meat and vegetables into small pieces and handed the plate back to Agnes.

Madame was talking to Sir Godfrey and did not look at her son.

After dinner, when they were washing up, Agnes said, 'Wonder what brings Mr Theo here? But he never stays long.'

'Why not?' said Caro. 'I suppose it's his home.'

'Not wanted in it,' Agnes said. 'Madame makes that quite clear, the old dragon. She never could abide him.'

'You're exaggerating, Agnes.'

'Oh, I am, am I?' said Agnes. 'I've heard her say with my own ears that she wished he'd never been born. It was when her little girl was dying of the 'flu that this one came, and she couldn't nurse the child herself because of him, and she always says it was because of him that she lost the girl. And then he was a queer one, which made it worse.'

'What do you mean, queer?' Matt asked.

'Well, you should see what his hand's like, and that arm which he keeps all covered up because she can't abide to see it.'

'What's wrong with it?'

'I've not seen it myself,' Agnes said. 'But they do say it's all nasty and deformed-like. The nurse told me Madame she went white as a sheet when they showed it to her first and she screamed out it couldn't be her child, and she wouldn't have it near her, not for anything. She never would touch him when he was a child.'

'That was very wrong,' Caro said gravely.

'It was worse when she had the other boy,' said Agnes with relish. 'Mr Julian, that was killed in the war, Alix's father. She took plenty of notice of him. Nothing was too good for Julian, and when they was older, he was always with his mother and Mr Theo had to keep out of the way, even had his meals in the schoolroom, or with us sometimes in the kitchen, for company or to save the trouble of carrying them, for he was ever so shy as a boy, never had a word to say for himself. Some do say he's not all there, but to me he seems just slow, like. He was terrible stupid at school, they say, couldn't go to college like his brother or that Jasper Hartnoll. And now you see Mr Julian's gone, and she's left with him, the one she never could take to.'

'Poor Mr Ayre,' said Matt. 'I like him.'

'You don't know him,' said Caro.

'Yes, I do,' said Matt.

He was inclined to take anyone's side against Madame.

Suddenly there was a violent crack of thunder: it seemed right over the house.

'Ow!' cried Agnes in a fright, clutching her throat.

Matt wanted to giggle; he didn't know how to stop himself.

Perhaps it was as much to save his face as anything that Caro said, 'Matt, do be a darling and run and pick up the rug and cushions that naughty Alix left on the lawn, before they get wet.'

'But I'm not to go in the garden.'

'Madame won't see you. It's quite dark now.'

It was pitch dark, as Matt found when he got outside. He switched on his torch to find the path through the shrubbery. Suddenly there was a dazzling flash and everything was illuminated in a light that took all the colours out. He saw house and terrace and lawn, and the rug left there, all as clear as a photograph, and then it was dark again, black, and he felt blinded. As he groped his way on he heard voices and peering up, saw people at a french window looking out at the storm, and hoped they could not see him.

A woman's decisive voice, Freda's, he felt sure, said, 'Close down? Best thing, I daresay. There's never been enough money, has there?'

'People do give money sometimes,' said Theo Ayre's slow husky voice.

'You won't get any from me, Theodore, if that's what you are hinting at,' said Sir Godfrey Hartnoll coldly.

'If I wanted that I would ask for it, not hint,' said Theo Ayre, and Matt thought he sounded annoyed.

Matt reached the rug and rolled it up, picking up the cushions, which were damp with dew. Heavy drops began to fall slowly round him.

'What's that on the lawn?' Freda said suddenly, in her loud piercing voice. 'There! It's a torch. Someone's poking about with a torch.'

'You'd better go and see who it is, Theo,' said Sir Godfrey.

'Probably Price,' said Theo.

Matt began to run. It was difficult, with so many things to carry, but he didn't want to be hauled into the drawing-room before Madame on his very first evening.

'He's running away!' cried Freda, giving chase at once, as if she were out beagling.

Theo came heavily after her.

Stumbling and running, Matt tripped over the trailing rug and fell headlong. The intrepid Freda pounced on him. 'It's a boy!' she cried. 'What are you doing here, I'd like to know?'

'I was only fetching the rug,' said Matt, breathlessly.

Theo came up. 'Is that you, Matt?'

'Yes,' said Matt, thankfully.

Theo laughed. 'I'm sorry we chased you,' he said, helping Matt to his feet. 'Here, give me some of that, I'll take it.'

'Who is he?' Freda asked suspiciously.

'He's Miss Rendal's brother. She is housekeeping for Mamma.'

A shout came from the terrace.

'Freda, do go and calm your father,' said Theo. 'I'll take these in at the back and come round.'

'Oh, very well,' said Freda crossly and went off, her taffeta dress swishing over the grass with an angry hiss.

Theo took most of the things from Matt. 'You light the way,' he said.

Flash! Everything shone out in a pink flare. Thunder rumbled and cracked overhead. Suddenly the rain came down, slapping on the ground as if enormous buckets were being emptied from the sky.

They hurried across the yard. Caro was standing in the doorway looking out for Matt. She had switched on the outside light and it shone down on her, illuminating her gold hair in its Grecian knot, her bare arms, her bright blue striped apron.

'Oh there you are!' she said, and then saw Matt was not alone. She moved back and Matt dived into the kitchen but Theo stood shyly outside in the rain, with the cushions and rug clasped under his arm.

'Come in, Mr Ayre,' said Caro, smiling. 'You'll get terribly wet if you don't! How kind of you to help Matt. You are Mr Ayre, aren't you?'

'Yes, thank you,' said Theo absurdly and squeezed through the door with his load and stood there shyer than ever, gazing at Caro as if he could not believe she was real.

Caro was never shy and she was only amused at his stupid behaviour. She took the rug and cushions from him and dumped them on a chair.

Agnes Orchard was still in the kitchen, in her coat and hat, waiting for the storm to stop. She was watching Mr Ayre, and gave a sniff, which diverted his attention from Caro at last.

'Hullo, Agnes,' he said. 'Shall I take you back home in the brake? It's a nasty night for bicycling.'

Agnes hesitated, giving him a sideways glance. 'Well, Mr Ayre, I thought you didn't have a licence,' she said.

'P.C. Carter won't be out in this,' said Theo. 'I can drive all right as far as the village, I assure you. We can put your bicycle in the back.'

The drenching sound of the rain decided Agnes. 'Well, thank you sir, very much,' she said doubtfully.

Theo went out again into the yard and presently they heard the car start up.

'I hope it's safe, all right,' Agnes said nervously.

'It's not far,' said Caro. 'And not a main road.'

When Theo brought the car round to the back door Matt noticed that he had his right hand out of the sling and resting on the wheel. There was a glove over it. But if he could use it, why keep it in a sling, Matt wondered.

Caro and Matt watched him drive Agnes away through the yard gates.

'He seems in control of it all right,' said Caro. She was never one to worry. She shut the back door.

'Well, don't you think he's nice too?' Matt said.

Caro laughed. 'I think he's rather funny, poor thing,' she said.

5

Nero Scared

THE next morning was fine and Matt went out in the woods, exploring. It was wet underfoot and he kept mostly to the paths, till he came out into a green grass ride that ran very straight each way between the trees. Looking down it, he saw the house at the end, in its circle of lawns and gardens, in its peaceful hollow of sunlight. Yet for all the peace Matt felt there was something a little sinister about the way it stood isolated like that, a place apart, a lonely place.

Looking up the other way he saw the white-pillared summerhouse, and thought he would go and look at it. The little dome was copper, and had turned turquoise green; there was a weather-vane on top of it: the wind was blowing softly from the south-west. Round the odd little tower at the back Matt could see strange signs, and he wanted to get a closer look at them. But he had not reached it when he heard a thudding on the ground, coming down from the ridge, and thought it sounded like a horse coming. He ran out from the lee of the summerhouse to look.

There was the horse, quite near, black Nero thundering down the ride with Mr Ayre on his back. Matt suddenly felt what it would be like to face a cavalry charge, the great horse seemed to be bearing down on him, turf flying from his galloping hooves. Matt gasped and jumped back, and as he did so a jay flew up in the woods, screeching danger. The black horse reared up with a screaming neigh of terror. Matt stared up open-mouthed at the sight, the horse on its hind legs, the front ones pawing the air, its eyes rolling and red with fright. Mr Ayre kept his seat the first time, but Nero reared again and he fell off. The horse bolted away down the ride, the stirrups swinging out loose from the saddle.

Theo Ayre sat up and rubbed his head and laughed.

'Oh dear, was that my fault?' Matt said anxiously, running towards him.

'Not altogether,' said Theo.

He was wearing old riding-breeches and a jersey and he looked more comfortable in them than in his evening dress last night. That had made him look fat and rather silly, but now Matt saw that he wasn't fat, only large. The size of everything about him made his deformed arm look very shrunken and feeble, almost like a child's arm inside the sleeve of his sweater, and by daylight Matt saw that the glove he wore was like a baby's, with no fingers.

Suddenly he saw that Mr Ayre had noticed him looking at his arm. Matt felt his face go hot, and knew it must be red.

'Don't feel embarrassed about my arm,' said Theo Ayre calmly. 'I'm quite used to everybody looking at it.'

Matt felt relieved at once. 'But please, why haven't you got it in a sling like you had last night?' he said. 'Does it hurt sometimes?'

'No, it doesn't hurt,' said Theo. 'I only wear it in a sling here because Mamma doesn't like to see it. That's why I couldn't manage my food properly last night, because I'm used to helping myself with this a bit. Thank you for cutting it up for me. It made it much easier.'

'Oh, did you see me?' Matt said.

Mr Ayre laughed. 'I saw you having a good look at us all,' he said. 'We must have been rather a depressing sight.' He got up from the ground. 'Well, I suppose I shall have to walk home now.'

'What will happen to Nero?' Matt asked.

'Oh, he'll probably go back to his stable,' said Theo Ayre.

Matt walked along beside him.

'Mr Ayre, please,' he said. 'Do you wear that glove because of Madame too?'

'No, I always wear that,' he answered. 'My hand isn't very nice to look at. It's not a proper hand, you know.'

Matt looked up at him thoughtfully.

'Do you mind about it very much, Mr Ayre?'

Mr Ayre did not answer at once, but after a moment he said, 'Sometimes I do. I try not to, but I can't say I like it when I see people looking either disgusted or pitying.'

'Don't you like them to be sorry for you?'

'No,' said Theo Ayre. 'The way most people are sorry for anyone is to treat him as somehow different from themselves, a poor thing, not a person.'

Matt thought how Caro had called him a poor thing last night, and felt guilty on her behalf.

'They don't think of course,' went on Mr Ayre. 'If they did they might realize that not having a body like theirs doesn't mean one doesn't have a mind and feelings like theirs.'

Matt remembered what Agnes had said about people believing that Mr Ayre was not quite 'all there' and thought he saw what he meant.

'But I suppose you would rather they were sorry than unkind,' he said, thinking about Madame's behaviour.

Theo Ayre looked at him. 'What do you mean, Matt?'

Matt flushed and did not know what to say. He muttered something about Agnes.

'I suppose Agnes has been talking away as usual,' said Mr Ayre, and he smiled, to Matt's relief. 'I know how she does, I remember it from years ago, when I was often in the kitchen, as a child. She likes to make a drama out of everything.'

'Isn't it true, then, that Madame was unkind to you, and liked your brother best?' Matt asked.

Theo was silent for a moment and then he said, 'Well, my brother was good-looking and clever, you know. People always did like him better, naturally.'

'Was he nice to you?' Matt asked.

There was such a long pause at this that he looked up and said, 'Shouldn't I ask so many questions?'

Theo Ayre smiled again. 'No, why shouldn't you? It's only that I don't want to be unfair to Julian, because he's dead and can't answer back. We didn't get on very well, but I daresay it was as much my fault as his. I can't say I was happy here as a child, because I wasn't, but I think now perhaps it was good for me to have something to struggle with, and learn how to bear things alone. If things are made too easy at first it's all the more difficult when you grow up and find the world won't alter itself to suit you.'

Matt walked along in silence, thinking this over. All the same, he had a feeling that Mr Ayre was making it sound much better than it had been. He imagined Julian Ayre rather like Jasper Hartnoll, but with that cool arrogance that had so much annoyed him when he first met Alix. It was not a very pleasant picture, and he was still firmly on the side of Theo Ayre.

'Are you staying long this time, Mr Ayre?' he asked.

'I don't know,' he answered. 'Don't call me Mr Ayre. I never feel much of a mister. The children always call me Theo.'

'What children?'

'In our school.'

'Oh, do you have a school?' Matt said. Aunt Maud must have been right, then.

'It's not my school really,' said Theo. 'It was started by my friend Sam Kingston and his wife Maggie. It's not an ordinary school. It's for children who are crippled or handicapped in ways that make it difficult for them to go to ordinary schools. Sam lets me help, though I'm not really clever enough to teach in a school. But there are lots of things to do besides teaching. Some of them need carrying about and there are always odd jobs to be done. The children like me to have this funny hand, because it makes them feel I'm like them, though I'm lucky compared with most of them.'

'Do you like looking after them?' Matt asked.

'Yes, very much,' said Theo and sighed. 'I'm worried about them now because we've got to leave the house we're in, and we were getting it at a very low rent, and we have very little money. I put in all I could when we started, but I haven't much of my own, it's tied up in this house and land and my mother has the use of what there is for her lifetime. Sam and Maggie have nothing of their own and only some of the children's parents can pay. Some haven't got any parents, anyway. It's getting very difficult indeed. I wish –' he stopped, looking down at the great house sitting there in the sun.

'What do you wish?' Matt asked.

'I wish they could come here,' said Theo. 'I wish I could let them have this house.'

'But can't you, as it's your house?'

Theo Ayre looked down at him with troubled eyes.

'Mamma would never consent.'

'Have you asked her?'

Theo shook his head. 'I must ask her,' he said. 'It's what I came to do. But it's very unlikely she will say yes. She is old now, and does not like things to be changed.'

'But if it's your own house?'

'Well, you know, Matt, it's only mine by law; it belongs to the family really, and that means Mamma now.'

'It would be a jolly thing if those crippled children came,' said Matt. 'It's much too empty, that house.'

'I think so too,' said Theo. 'Have you met my niece Alix?'

Matt could not help giggling.

'What's funny?' Theo asked, smiling.

'Just to think you're her uncle. You're so unlike her.'

'I'm not like the others in my family at all,' said Theo, with a sigh. 'I'm the misfit, throwback, or whatever you call it. So you have met Alix? Don't you think it's wrong for a girl to live here all alone with only old women to look after her? What do you think of her?'

'I think she behaves like a princess in a fairy story,' said Matt.

Theo laughed. 'Yes, she does! But I'm afraid ordinary life isn't much like a fairy story, and she may hurt herself when she goes out into the world, and probably other people too. You must come and play with her, do things with her.'

'I can't,' said Matt. 'Madame has forbidden me to go into the house, or the garden.'

Theo was silent for a moment and then he said, 'I see,' in a very slow way, as if he did not like his mother's command, but was not surprised by it. Then he added cheerfully, 'Well, we must have some picnics in the woods, then. Perhaps your sister will come. What is her name, her Christian name?'

'Caroline,' said Matt. 'But I call her Caro.'

'Caro,' he said slowly and walked along in silence for some time.

'Did you like Caro?' said Matt hopefully.

'I've never seen anyone so beautiful in my life,' said Theo solemnly.

Matt was pleased. 'She's nice as well,' he said.

'I'm sure she is,' said Theo.

They came back to the stable yard and there was Nero, standing quite quiet, and Caro was holding his bridle and talking to him.

'Hullo,' she said to them. 'He came back in a dreadful state of nerves. What happened?'

Theo seemed struck dumb again at the sight of her, so Matt related the incident. Price came into the yard and took Nero off to rub him down.

'You don't come often enough to ride him, sir, that's the trouble,' he said and walked off, as if he were afraid he might have to say more if he stayed.

Matt began to tell Caro that they were to have a picnic in the woods and that she was to come too.

'It will have to be on my afternoon off, then,' she said, laughing. 'And now I must go and make coffee for Madame. Shall I put a cup on the tray for you, Mr Ayre?'

'No thank you,' he said, coming to life again.

'Don't you like coffee?' Matt asked.

'Yes, I do, but Mamma doesn't like me to have it with her,' said Theo calmly.

'Good gracious!' said Caro, gazing at him in surprise. 'Well, would you like to have some somewhere else?'

She made coffee.

'Yes please, I'll have it in here,' said Theo, following her into the kitchen.

Caro laughed, but she did not make any objection. She made the coffee and Agnes took the tray away, and Caro handed cups to Theo and Matt and took one herself.

Theo did not seem to be going to say anything at all, so Matt began to tell Caro about the school, but she was busy, and hardly listened except to say, 'And what's it called?'

'St Raphael's School,' said Theo.

'That's nice,' said Caro. 'St Raphael is my favourite Archangel, I sometimes think. Looking after Tobias was such a homely thing for an Archangel to do. Now I must get on with the lunch, so you'd better both go away.'

She spoke as if Theo and Matt were both the same size and age. Theo went meekly away into the house and Matt went off to watch Price.

6

Bertrand's Tower

In the afternoon Matt went out into the wood and wandered, almost without meaning to, towards the old blue door in the wall that led to the rose garden. He bent down and peered through the keyhole, but of course he could only see the flowers, and the box borders, and the dark yew hedge. He sighed.

A laugh sounded in the wood behind him.

Matt turned round but no one was there. The light dappled the ground, dappled the brambles under the trees, midges danced in the slanting sunbeams. A shiver ran up his spine. Surely he *had* heard a laugh?

Then a green acorn hit him on the shoulder. He looked up and saw Alix in the oak tree, laughing down at him. She was barefoot and wore a green dress, so that her eyes looked greener than ever.

'You did look scared!' she said. 'Come up here.'

Matt climbed up into the oak, swinging himself on to the lowest branch. Alix laughed and climbed one higher. So he went after her, and they scrambled up each side of the stem till the boughs grew too thin to carry them farther. It seemed as if the sky was just above them, blue and full of sun.

'I'm glad you've come back,' said Alix.

'You weren't at dinner last night,' said Matt.

'No, it was a grown-ups' dinner. I didn't care because I hate all the Hartnolls. Aunt Phyllis is silly and the others are horrid. Freda is always telling me I ought to play hockey, as if I could by myself! How did you know I wasn't there?'

'I took the plates at the hatch for Agnes,' said Matt. 'I cut up the meat for Theo, too.'

'You ought to call him Mr Ayre,' said Alix.

'He told me to call him Theo,' said Matt, triumphantly.

'Oh did he? Well, I don't like him either,' said Alix. 'He's stupid. Gran'mère says he couldn't do the simplest lessons. My father was always much cleverer, although he was two years younger. I bet I know more than Uncle Theo does now.'

'All the same, he teaches in a school,' said Matt. 'He told me so.'

'Teaches poor little idiots not to pick their noses,' said Alix.

'They're not idiots, they're cripples,' said Matt.

'Like Uncle Theo,' said Alix. 'It must be nasty to be so ugly but Gran'mère says he's too stupid to care. I wonder what his hand looks like when he takes his glove off? I suppose he has to take it off to wash.'

Matt said nothing but he began to climb down the tree.

'Where are you going?' Alix asked anxiously.

'Away,' said Matt briefly.

'Oh, Matt! Why?'

'Because you're being so nasty about Theo, and I like him,' said Matt.

'Oh don't be silly, Matt!' Alix cried. 'I like him too sometimes.'

A gust of wind shook the tree suddenly. The boughs swayed and shivered under the children and all the leaves round began to rustle and sigh.

'Wind!' said Alix, her eyes shining. 'Come on, let's go to the pine place.'

Hand over hand she came down the tree like a monkey, passing Matt and dropping to the ground first. She ran off up a path through the wood, still barefoot, and he ran after her.

Presently the ground was all netted with pine needles and they were running uphill. Alix stopped on a little knoll and turned round. Tall red pine stems stood straight up round them like masts, swaying in the new wind.

'Listen!' said Alix.

The pine trees were sighing. Through all their million million green needles the air ran fast and slow, and the trees breathed a sound like the sea, softly flowing and hushing far round them, far above.

'It's like the sea,' Matt said at last.

'The sea!' Alix said. 'Have you seen the sea?'

'Haven't you?' said Matt, astonished.

'Oh no, never!' Alix said. 'I so much want to. But I have never been away from here and this is in the middle of England, you know, it's almost the farthest from the sea that you can be in England.'

'Never been away from here?' Matt repeated.

'Never,' said Alix, sadly. 'Gran'mère never goes away.'

A stronger blast of wind came rushing through the wood and the sound of the pines rose louder, a soft roaring in their ears.

Alix suddenly shut her eyes, listening, and Matt watched that listening face, drawn away from earth by the strange sound. For it was somehow a stranger sound than the sea: the murmur of the trees lulled in their ears, whispering of remoter shores, infinite regions, another world, a world without people.

'It makes me want to die,' Alix said in a whisper, opening her eyes, and they looked as if she had gone far away, her green eyes, usually so light and piercing.

'To die?' Matt echoed her, uncertainly.

'To go away and away and away and never come back,' said Alix. 'I love it!'

'Well, I don't want to die,' said Matt firmly.

'Nor do I, really,' said Alix, coming back to earth. 'It's just a feeling. Come on.'

Off she went again, over the knoll and on, leaving the mysterious pines to their sighing solitude. Matt caught her up.

'Where are you going?' he said.

'I don't know. Where would you like?'

Their path opened suddenly into the ride where Matt had met Theo riding his black horse that morning.

'I'd like to see the summer-house,' he said, looking towards it. 'Can you go inside?' He saw that it was bigger than he thought; distance had diminished it.

'We don't call it a summer-house,' said Alix.

'What do you call it?'

'Bertrand's Tower.'

Matt looked at it again; a blue shadow leant out from it across the grass.

'Why is it called that?'

'Because Bertrand built it,' said Alix, as they walked over the green grass in the hot late July afternoon. 'He was an ancestor of ours who lived in sixteen-something and he built it to look at the stars.'

They stood in front of the portico and Matt saw there were words in Latin round the cornice above the pillars.

BENEDICITE LUX ET TENEBRAE DOMINO

'Light and shadow bless the Lord,' he said slowly, working it out.

They went up the shallow stone steps and Alix opened the door into the tower. Inside, rather to Matt's disappointment, was a room full of old deck-chairs, folding tables, and all sorts of junk, including a rusty army bed and a shelf of musty books.

'Why is there such a lot of stuff?' he asked.

'I believe Uncle Theo used to come up here often when he lived at Woodhall,' said Alix. 'Slept here too, sometimes.'

'All by himself? How peculiar,' said Matt.

'Well, he is peculiar, I told you so,' said Alix. 'But some of this stuff has been here for years and years, since before the First World War, Price told me.'

A narrow winding stair climbed out of this room full of junk and up this they soon went, coming out in a small low room, where there was a great yellowed sphere standing in the centre. Matt went up to look, and saw it was drawn all over with the constellations, figured as classical people and formal animals.

'What is it?' he asked, staring at it.

'A celestial globe,' said Alix. She made it turn with her hands.

'This has been here ever since Bertrand went away.'

'Since he died?'

'No, since he went,' said Alix.

The room was rather dim, lit only by slits all round, and Matt said, with a prickly feeling in his neck, 'What do you mean?'

'Well, he went into exile with James II,' said Alix. 'He fought in the battle of the Boyne and was wounded there and then he went to St Germains in France with the King, and when the King went on retreat to the Cistercians at La Trappe Bertrand went too and he decided to stay there and be a monk. So he died in La Trappe.'

'And never came back?'

'No, and all the family here turned Protestant because it was less trouble and they didn't have to pay fines then. It wasn't till Grandfather married Gran'mère that they became Catholic again. He did it to please her.'

'And now she doesn't even go to mass!' said Matt.

'Because Rosario died,' said Alix, twirling the globe.

'Did your grandfather lapse too?' Matt asked.

'Oh no,' said Alix. 'He was much more pious than she ever was, in the end, Price says. Price was always a Catholic and used to pray for Grandfather's conversion. It was Grandfather had the chapel made, and he found the statue that used to be on the fountain, he bought it somewhere abroad.'

'I wonder where it is now?' Matt said. 'Did your grandfather make the Rose Round too?'

'No,' said Alix. 'That was there. I think it was made by Bertrand too, for a lady he wanted to marry, but then her father wouldn't let her because he was on William's side, William the Third. He married her off to somebody else and she became a Duchess and knew Marlborough and all those people.'

'Poor Bertrand,' said Matt. 'He seems to have had a hard sort of life.'

'Let's go on the roof,' said Alix.

'Can we?'

'Of course. That's what it's for, an observatory.'

They climbed up an old wooden ladder and through a small door, set aslant, almost like a trap-door, and then they were on the leaded roof. The lead was hot to their feet and Alix, without shoes, had to dance about till she found a patch of shade behind the door to stand on. The top of the tower was enclosed by the parapet, waist high and twelve-sided. In the middle was a great circular dial engraved on bronze, with a curly gnomon standing up to point the hour. Its shadow lay black and sharp in the hot afternoon sun.

'Words round the sundial too,' said Matt, bending down to look.

'Yes, do you know what they mean? I don't.'

'LUX UMBRA DEI,' Matt slowly read out.

'Not those,' said Alix. 'That's easy. "Light is the shadow of God," that means. No, it's the ones underneath I can't make out.'

'Light is the shadow of God,' Matt repeated, and squinted towards the sun. 'How can light be a shadow?'

'Listen,' said Alix, and she read the inscription at the base of the dial, tracing the letters with her finger. 'PEREUNT ET IMPUTANTUR. What does that mean?'

Matt did not know. The words teased them, promising meaning and withholding it.

'Did people know much about the stars in those days?' Matt said.

'Of course they did. Think of Newton,' said Alix. 'Bertrand met him. He knew all those people, Fellows of the Royal Society and so on. He was a scientist himself in his way, a Natural Philosopher, they called it then. But the funny thing is, that although he was so clever and Theo is so stupid, he looks like Theo, only not so ugly, and he has two proper hands of course.'

'How do you know what he looks like?' Matt said, leaning on the parapet and gazing towards the house, that looked from here like a big red dolls' house sitting in its hollow of green.

'From his portrait, silly,' said Alix. 'It's in the Library.'

'I suppose he used to stand here and look at the house like this,' said Matt pensively.

'No, he didn't,' said Alix. 'At least, if he did the house didn't look the same. It was rebuilt by his brother in the next reign. His brother married an heiress and did well for himself.'

'But they left his tower,' said Matt. 'And the Rose Round.'

'Yes,' said Alix. 'Oh, there's Mademoiselle coming. I must go. I've got a music lesson with Mr Howell after tea.'

They went downstairs to the dim room where the celestial sphere stood, and then down through the junk and out on to the grass again. Matt saw a small black figure advancing up the ride ringing a hand-bell vigorously.

'What shall I do?' he said nervously.

'Oh, never mind Mademoiselle, she's quite harmless,' said Alix. 'I can make her do whatever I like. Besides, you're not in the garden here.' She skipped down to meet the old lady. 'Mademoiselle Tousselin, this is Matthew Rendal.'

'Mon Dieu, Alix, but your Grandemère said you were not to play wid zis boy,' said Mademoiselle, agitated, blinking helplessly at Matt.

She was a thin wrinkled old woman with a black velvet band round her throat. It was clasped with a large cameo representing Andromache saying farewell to Hector. Her hair was black and strained back in a tight bun. She was dressed entirely in black.

'No, Toussie, she only said he was not to come in the garden. Now, Toussie, don't be naughty,' said Alix, twining her arms ingratiatingly round the old woman's neck. 'If you tell I'll never love you any more.'

'Alix, you have taken off your shoes again,' said Mademoiselle. 'Hélas! When will you learn to be a young lady?'

'When I am one,' said Alix, laughing.

'Now come back, bad girl,' said Mademoiselle, smiling. 'Tea is ready, and soon will come Mr Hovelle.'

'Howell, Toussie, not Hovelle!' cried Alix, bursting into peals of laughter. 'Good-bye, Matt! I'll see you again.' And off she went, trying to make the protesting little Frenchwoman run down the slope.

Later that evening Matt heard the harp, its twangling runs echoing through the summer evening. He leaned over the paddock gate, listening, and thinking of Bertrand's Tower, and his story, the things that had happened here so long ago. The human lady for whom the rose garden had been made had never come to Woodhall as a bride, and the statue of the heavenly lady had been thrown away and lost. Bertrand Ayre had died in the silence of La Trappe, and little Rosario had died here in this house when Theo was born, but the roses were still growing in the garden and the tower still stood which the young philosopher had built to look at the stars.

'Perhaps history is all like that,' Matt thought. 'People coming and going, things being built and vanishing, and only the sun going on the same, telling the hours on top of the tower.'

The sun was going down in the sky now; he could look at it without blinking.

'*Lux umbra Dei*,' he repeated to himself. Perhaps God

was so bright that even the sun was only a shadow to him.

Alix stopped playing the harp and silence fell. The wind had dropped away. Everything was still.

Matt remembered that he had never looked at the signs on the twelve sides of the tower.

7

Trouble for Theo

AFTER that Matt saw Alix nearly every day. It had never occurred to Madame, when she forbade Matt the house, that her granddaughter would then seek her new friend in the stables and the kitchen, but of course she did. She soon gave up her initial suspicion of Caro and pestered her with questions about dresses, poring over magazines that Agnes used to bring up to the house for her spare moments. She and Matt ranged the woods or, if it was wet, played wild games in the rambling outbuildings, defending sack castles against fearful odds, or dying on hayloft quarterdecks.

Alix was not the only visitor to the backstairs regions. Theo seemed to find a lot to do in the yard, or in the stables. Among other things he began to teach Matt to ride.

'Though perhaps you won't think I am much of a teacher after what you saw at Bertrand's Tower,' he said.

'What did he see at Bertrand's Tower?' Alix asked at once.

'Me falling off Nero,' said Theo.

All the same he was a good teacher, patient and unruffled whatever happened. Matt learned to ride Alix's pony, Primrose, but when he got more confident Theo transferred him to Price's bigger pony, Gipsy, so that they could all go out together. Matt loved it, although at first he got very stiff and sore. But to be able to ride a horse had been one of his ambitions for years, and now he could. It was a triumph and a satisfaction.

Theo often seemed to come into the kitchen just when Caro was making tea or coffee or cocoa, and so he drank a good many cups of all these, one way and another. Caro always treated him in a friendly way, but very much as if he were one of the children. He never said very much to her, though he talked quite a lot when he was out with Matt and Alix.

At last Theo succeeded in organizing his picnic, but they did not go in the woods, they went to Ludlow to see the castle. Caro could not refuse to come, because she had to drive the brake, since Theo had no licence. On this expedition Theo was wearing a tweed jacket, and although he did not have his sling, Matt noticed that he kept his right hand most of the time in his pocket.

It was a sunny, windy August afternoon and everyone loved Ludlow. Alix was quite wild with excitement and the fun of being out without even Mademoiselle to watch her. She sang at the top of her voice, coming home, bouncing about in the back of the car, French songs and English songs and even a Welsh song Mr Howell had taught her to sing to the harp.

'My mother was Welsh,' she said proudly. 'Could she speak Welsh, Uncle Theo?'

'Oh yes, and sing in it,' he said.

'How did Father meet her?' Alix wanted to know. 'Did he go to Wales?'

'No,' said Theo. 'I went to Wales. I asked Helen to come and stay at Woodhall, and Julian was on leave. They were married in a few weeks.'

'How romantic!' said Alix.

'So Madame approved of her,' Caro said.

'I'm not sure she did,' said Theo. 'But Julian could always get round Mamma.'

'Why did you go to Wales, Theo?' Matt asked.

'It was in the war, you know,' he said. 'I went all over the place, then.'

'But you weren't in the army or anything, were you?' said Alix. 'Gran'mère said you couldn't do anything in the war because of your arm.'

'I wasn't allowed to do most of the things I tried to do,' said Theo. 'That was when I first met Sam Kingston and began to work with the children. First of all it was evacuees. Sam had a home for the bad boys, whom everyone else threw out. We had a wild time with them! Funny as well, sometimes. I had a letter from one of them yesterday, who went to Canada. He's just got married; that makes me feel very old.'

'You don't look old, Theo,' said Matt kindly and Theo laughed.

'I've got some grey hairs all the same,' he said.

Alix, not liking to be out of the limelight, said, 'Was my mother beautiful, Uncle Theo.'

'Yes.'

'What sort of beautiful? Dark, like me?'

'Ha, ha! Beautiful!' Matt jeered. 'You're not beautiful.'

'I'm going to be, Gran'mère said so,' said Alix, annoyed. 'She says I am going to break hearts.'

'I hope not,' said Theo.

'I shouldn't mind breaking a few,' said Alix. 'Not nice people's hearts, of course.'

'Unfortunately you can't choose who is going to fall in love with you,' said Caro. 'It's always rather worrying, whether they're nice or not.'

'People are always falling in love with Caro,' said Matt boastfully.

Caro laughed. 'Shut up, Matt!'

'Well, they are. All the young masters at the schools you've worked in. Not only the young ones, either.'

'Matt, you don't know anything about it,' said Caro.

Matt chuckled. 'Oh, don't I?' he said.

'The next turning is ours, Miss Rendal,' said Theo.

'Why do you always call her Miss Rendal?' said Matt. 'Why don't you call her Caro?'

Theo laughed. 'It wouldn't be polite unless she asked me to.'

'Well! Of course you would rather he called you Caro, wouldn't you, Caro?' said Matt.

'Oh goodness, I don't mind,' said Caro, carelessly.

Not long after the Ludlow trip Caro said to Matt, 'Jasper's coming down to his home and I'm going to see him on my next day off. He's still frightened of my running into his father while I'm working here, so we're meeting in Kidderminster, of all places.'

In the afternoon when she came down to go out, a week after Ludlow, Theo and Matt were just about to go for a ride. Alix was not there; she was having a music lesson. Caro came out into the yard looking very smart in her best dress of red silk, with a white coat and sandals and little white hat. She was wearing her engagement ring for the first time at Woodhall, a very brilliant one which flashed in the sun as she patted Gipsy's neck.

'Be good, Matt, and don't pester Mr Ayre too much.'

'Be good yourself,' he retorted, and she went off laughing, waving as she went through the gate.

When Theo and Matt came through it, she was already half-way down the drive, a small gay figure walking quickly between the dappling lime trees.

Theo looked after her and then said slowly, 'She was wearing a ring today.'

'It's her engagement ring,' said Matt gloomily.

Theo turned his face to him and it was quite pale, Matt noticed with surprise.

'Is she going to be married?' he said, and it sounded as if he liked the idea quite as little as Matt himself.

'Yes, but I mustn't say who to,' said Matt. 'He may be rich, but I don't like him and I can't think why she does, except that he looks like a film star and has a Jaguar.'

Theo said nothing for a moment, and then, as they went slowly along a ride through the woods he asked, 'But if he's rich, why is she working? Why don't they get married at once?'

'Because his father doesn't think Caro is good enough for them,' said Matt. 'Old beast!'

'I don't think much of the son, then,' said Theo. 'That wouldn't stop me very long!'

Matt said, 'You sound as if you would like to marry Caro yourself.'

Theo said, 'I would.'

Matt gazed at him with his mouth open.

'Not really?' he said at last.

Theo looked at him and said, 'Don't tell anyone that, will you? It slipped out by mistake.'

'But is it true?'

'Yes, why shouldn't it be true?' said Theo. 'Or do you think anyone as ugly as I am, and with a misshapen arm like this, has no business to fall in love with a girl like Caro? It is ridiculous, I know. But I can't help it, Matt, you can't help that sort of thing.'

'I'd much rather she married you than Ja—' Matt stopped just in time.

Theo smiled, not very happily. 'That's very kind of you, Matt,' he said and sighed. 'Well, I knew it was no good hoping, all along, but now I must make up my mind to it. Don't tell anyone.'

'Not even Caro?'

'No, no,' said Theo in alarm. 'For heaven's sake, Matt!'

'Why not?' said Matt. 'She's quite used to people falling in love with her. She may have guessed already, she usually does.'

'I hope not,' said Theo anxiously. 'But if nothing's said she can pretend she hasn't guessed, and then it won't be a worry to her.'

'Oh, it wouldn't worry her,' Matt assured him.

Theo squeezed up his mouth as if he suddenly had toothache and then said, 'No, why should it? It wouldn't mean anything to her that I loved her.'

He urged Nero forward in a canter and Matt went after him on Gipsy, trying to remember everything he had been taught.

When Caro returned she came and sat on Matt's bed.

'Did you have a nice time?' he asked, dutifully.

'Yes and no,' said Caro. 'Jasper was maddening at first about my being here, but finally I've convinced him his father can't possibly guess, and so he's going to come over sometimes, Jasper, I mean. But we didn't have so much fun as we used to in Birmingham, somehow.'

Matt, who had never had fun with Jasper, said, 'Coming to see you?'

'Well, yes, but we must pretend not to have met before,' said Caro. 'Isn't it funny?'

Matt thought it was stupid, but did not say so.

Sure enough, a day or two later Jasper Hartnoll turned up at Woodhall. He called on Mrs Ayre, who was his aunt by marriage, gave his little cousin Alix a silk scarf which delighted her, and cleverly got her to take him, before he left, through the green baize door to be introduced to Caro and Matt. Although Caro was twinkling a little, you could never have told they knew each other already.

Theo happened to be in the kitchen, having a cup of tea, and Jasper, perhaps to make it easier for Caro, talked mostly to him, or at him, for he teased him all the time.

'Hullo, Theo,' he said. 'They must feed their benefactors well at the cripples' home. You look at least a hundredweight heavier than when I last saw you. Or is it all the result of Miss Rendal's wonderful cooking?'

'She certainly cooks very well,' said Theo.

'You'll have to be careful, Theo,' said Jasper solemnly, 'Or one day when you come home the floor will give way and you'll disappear into the cellar.'

Alix burst out laughing.

'He's already broken one of the Chippendale chairs,' she said.

'You'll have to lay in some iron chairs,' Jasper said, leaning against the dresser and laughing at Theo, who said nothing, but went on eating one of Caro's buns. All the same Matt felt he didn't like being teased so much about his weight.

'Steady with the buns!' said Jasper. 'Old age is creeping up on you, Theo. Forty shows up the greed of twenty.'

'I'm not forty,' said Theo.

'You must be near it,' said Jasper. 'You're ten years older than me and I'm twenty-eight.'

'Caro's twenty-eight,' said Matt.

'Hey, you mustn't give away a girl's age like that!' Jasper said.

'Will you have some tea, Mr Hartnoll?' said Caro politely, but her eyes were bright with amusement.

Jasper accepted the tea with a bow, although he had already had some with Madame in the drawing-room. Both he and Caro evidently found it funny to pretend not to know each other, but it irritated Matt and he wished Jasper would go away. He had to, in the end, but after that day he could not keep away from Woodhall. In the afternoons his Jaguar was nearly always in the yard except on Caro's day off, when, as Matt knew, he met her farther away and they went out together. Theo several times tried to arrange another trip like the one to Ludlow, but Caro always had this mysterious prior engagement.

So the days of August went on much the same, Matt and Alix playing in the wood, building a hut in the oak tree near the door to the garden, or riding, usually with Theo. Only now Jasper always seemed to be about, and as he did not dare to spend all his time with Caro the others often had to put up with him.

Matt hated him worse than ever at Woodhall, mostly because of the way he teased Theo. He was Theo's cousin, but he was much younger, and Matt wondered if he had dared to be so cheeky when he was a boy. He could not see Theo without jeering at his size or his stupidness, or the way he let his mother run Woodhall, and though Theo hardly ever retaliated, Matt could see he did not like it.

Alix, to Matt's disgust, rather admired Jasper.

'He's so terribly handsome,' she said. 'And he does say nice things and give lovely presents.' For Jasper continued to bring her pretty things, almost whenever he came. He brought flowers, too, for Madame, from his father's green-houses, and made her light-hearted compliments which pleased and flattered the old lady.

'You are like your father, Jasper,' she said once. 'But you have not his weight, I fear.'

'I leave weight to Theo, Tante Louise,' said Jasper.

Alix told Matt this, giggling.

'Why is he so nasty to Theo?' Matt said.

'He only teases him,' said Alix. 'After all, Theo is rather a stupid old thing. It makes Gran'mère laugh when Jasper makes rings round old Theo.'

'Yes, and he jolly well knows it will,' said Matt crossly.

'Theo doesn't mind. Everybody always teases him. My father used to, and Jasper used to follow my father round and copy him, Mademoiselle told me that.'

'He does mind,' said Matt. 'I think your father was nasty to him, just as nasty as he could be.'

'Don't be silly,' said Alix. 'Brothers always tease each other. Theo didn't mind.'

'Why did he go up to Bertrand's Tower by himself, then?' Matt said. 'Everyone was beastly to him, I know they were.'

'Oh, you take his side because you think you're like him,' cried Alix. 'Just like Gran'mère said when she first saw you.'

'I don't!' said Matt, who had never thought of it. But then after a moment he said, 'I wouldn't at all mind being like him. He's always the same and never gets in a temper.'

'He's too stupid to get in a temper,' said Alix, crossly. 'He's like a fat lazy old horse who can't go at more than a walk.'

'Oh, shut up!' Matt said.

'Shut up yourself!'

They glared at each other, and then Alix flounced off into the garden where Matt was not allowed to go.

8

More Trouble

THE next afternoon Alix had to go to the dentist. Price drove her in the Rolls and Mademoiselle went with her. She was looking at her most haughty and disdainful and Matt, who had been prepared to be sympathetic, made a face at her instead. Alix sailed off in the Rolls with her nose in the air.

Matt, left to himself, thought he would try a little stalking in the shrubbery. It was a hot afternoon, and pleasant under the shade of the shiny laurels. It was hardly worth stalking Madame, a mere old lady, however intimidating, so Matt pretended that the house was held by hostile Roundheads, and must at all costs be regained for the King. It was his ancestral home for the moment, rather than Theo's, and if he could retake it, single-handed, perhaps the King himself would knight him. 'Rise, Sir Matthew Rendal,' he murmured to himself, worming his way over the brown twiggy earth. A sharp stick dug into his ribs. 'Wounded!' he muttered, clutching his side. Of course that made his task all the harder and more glorious. He dragged himself painfully along, leaving, he was sure, a trail of blood. At last he almost reached the edge of the lawn and raised himself on his elbow, peering out through the fringe of leaves.

Suddenly Madame came out on to the terrace, only a few yards away. Although she was only an old lady Matt was quite as alarmed as if she had been the Roundhead general himself. He lay rigid, staring out at her. Theo came out after her and they both came down the steps to the lawn and Madame sat down on a wooden seat, hardly any distance away.

Matt held his breath, not daring to move.

'Well, Théo,' said Madame, resting her small white hands on the silver head of her ebony cane. 'Tell me what is on your mind.'

Theo sat down on the end of the bench, which gave a loud crack. He jumped up again at once.

'In any case you know I don't like you to sit that side of me,' said his mother sharply. 'Why are you not wearing the sling?'

'I'm sorry, Mamma, I forgot to put it on,' said Theo, hastily pushing his gloved hand into his trouser pocket. It was so hot he had not got a jacket on, and although his shirt had long sleeves it did not camouflage his arm so well.

'You should wear it all the time,' said Madame. 'It is unfair to other people that they should have to see this.'

'I'm sorry,' Theo said again.

Matt wondered why he didn't get cross. There Madame sat, so little and frail, just bullying Theo, who could almost have picked her up with his one hand, Matt thought.

'Well,' said Madame impatiently. 'What is this you wish to ask me? Don't be so slow about it. I do not find your company so stimulating that I wish to spend all the afternoon with you.'

Theo looked as if he did not know how to begin. He was standing in front of her now, and nervously rubbed his chin with his hand.

'Don't do that!' said his mother irritably. 'You haven't shaved today, either.'

'I have, Mamma.'

'Nonsense. I can see the beard from here.'

'It grows awfully quickly,' said Theo gloomily. 'I'll shave again before dinner, if you like.'

'Certainly you will, Théo. It's disgusting so. You look like a tramp.'

She had reduced him to silence again, but after a moment she said impatiently, 'Get on, get on. What is this important question? Must you take all day to ask it?'

'It's about the school, Mamma,' said Theo, desperately. 'There's nowhere for us to go. Sam's at his wits' end.'

'You know I have no money to spare for such things.'

'It's not money we want, Mamma, it's a roof over our heads. What I was thinking was –' he hesitated and then went on quickly. 'This house is so big, couldn't – couldn't we have part of it for the children?'

'Bring your little imbeciles to Woodhall? What an idea!' cried Madame.

'They're not imbeciles, Mamma.'

'Cripples, it's just as bad! How can you ask that of me, you who know what distress it has always caused me to see you, my eldest son, crippled as you are? It is like your senselessness to demand such a thing of your mother.'

'But Mamma, you would hardly see them,' Theo pleaded. 'We could use the back stairs and the rooms on that side and leave the best part of the house entirely to you. After all, we only have thirty children at present.'

'Thirty! Mon Dieu! Do you want to kill me? Put this mad idea out of your mind, Théodore.'

'But Mamma, if we can't find a rent-free house we shall have to close St Raphael's.'

'Rent free! Yes, that is what your Mr Kingston wants,'

said Madame. 'Can't you see how they use you, these vulgar people?'

'Sam and Maggie are my best friends,' Theo said. 'They've been very kind to me, kindest of anyone.' His voice shook.

'Yes! Of course!' cried Madame. 'They know how to flatter you and make you feel yourself someone important instead of the burden you have always been to your unfortunate family.'

Theo turned away abruptly and walked off a few paces across the lawn.

'Stop!' cried Madame. 'Where are you going? Why do you go off like that while I am speaking to you? Have you no manners at all?'

Theo paused, irresolute, half-turning back.

'I know why you go away,' she said. 'Because you don't like to hear the truth about your common friends, you like to think they love you so much for nothing. Pff! Ridiculous!'

'Don't!' said Theo, his voice gone hoarse, angry and miserable. 'You know nothing about my friends. You've no right to say things like that.'

'How dare you speak to your mother in that way!' cried the old lady, outraged, but perfectly in control of the situation, sure she was right. 'It's for your own good I tell you these things. This Sam thinks you are rich because you live in a big house, he says to his wife, "Be nice to this fool and we shall do well."'

'Please don't,' Theo said huskily. 'Let's say no more. Let's go in now, Mamma.'

He came a step or two back towards her.

'You are weeping, you great cry-baby,' said Madame, scornfully. 'Always tears, from a tiny child. Weeping be-

76

cause I won't let you be made a fool of, giving your house' our house, to a couple of common baby farmers.'

'Mamma, it's for the children,' Theo said. 'They have nowhere to go.'

'Rubbish!' said Madame. 'They are not coming here.'

Theo hesitated. Matt saw it was true, there were tears in his eyes, but he was not actually crying. He stood looking at his mother in silence for a moment. At last he said, very quietly, 'Aren't you afraid that our Lord will say to us: "I was homeless and you did not take me in?"'

'Don't you preach to me, Théodore,' his mother said, indignantly, rising to her feet and speaking in a sharp quivering voice. 'Let the good God look after those he has allowed to come into the world so twisted and deformed! He took from me my perfect child, my innocent: let him take these, whom nobody wants. What has God suffered that I should do anything for him?'

Theo stood facing her. He said, 'You know he suffered it all, both as Father and as Child.'

Mamma was absolutely silent, her face white and still. For a moment Matt thought she was going to admit she was wrong and agree to Theo's plan. But then she stiffened and drew herself upright, as if she were ashamed of her emotion, and said coldly, 'I dislike sermons in the afternoon, especially from my son. I will go in now. No, I do not want your help. I do not want your company. Go back to your horses, they have the same intellectual level.'

She walked up the steps, stiff and erect, and into the house.

Theo flung himself face down on the grass.

It was such a gesture of misery and defeat that Matt did not know what to do. He thought Theo might not like to know he had seen him lying there crying, so he kept quiet, although he was beginning to feel very damp underneath and twigs were sticking painfully into his stomach and thighs.

But suddenly he sneezed.

Theo started up as if he had been shot.

'Theo, it's only me,' Matt said, scrambling up to his knees and parting the leaves. 'I'm awfully sorry. I was stalking the house, and when you began talking I didn't dare move.'

'You heard everything then?' Theo said, coming and kneeling down and looking in at him.

'Yes. I am sorry, Theo. I'm sorry Madame was so un-kind.'

'She thinks she knows best,' said Theo, without much conviction.

'Why is she so horrible to you, Theo?'

Theo hesitated. 'I don't think she always realizes how much words can hurt,' he said at last. 'She's used to saying just what she pleases. It's one of the bad things about living here alone, ordering everyone about. She forgets to consider other people. And of course I always have irritated her. It's not only because of my hand. She loved the other two so much, the child she lost, and Julian, who was like her. When you get old you get set in your ways, ways of thinking too, and ways of treating people. To her I'm still a stupid boy who can't be trusted to manage any-thing without making a mess of it.'

'Well, I think it's very unfair,' said Matt.

Theo smiled and rubbed the tears from his face with his sleeve.

'It's nice of you to be so friendly, Matt,' he said. 'The boys I used to know would have laughed at me for crying like that.'

'I always thought people didn't cry when they were grown up,' said Matt. 'Not men, anyway.'

'Well, now you know some do, sometimes,' said Théo, with half a laugh, but he still did not look very happy.

'Come and have tea in the kitchen,' suggested Matt, wanting to cheer him up.

But Theo shook his head.

'I think I'll go for a walk,' he said. 'I'll walk up to Bertrand's Tower.'

He went away across the lawn and climbed over the bent, rusty iron fence that divided it from the parkland. Matt, watching, saw him slowly ascending the green central ride, towards the white tower, built so many years ago by the man who wanted to look at the stars and ended by looking at God alone.

Theo had not said anything about not telling anyone what had happened, and Matt soon found he could not keep it all to himself. He did not give away the fact that Madame had made Theo cry, but he told Caro of Theo's plan to bring the school to Woodhall.

'I wouldn't have expected anything so practical of him,' she said. 'He seems so passive, always. Well, the school will have to find a benefactor with more money, that's all, and no tyrannical Mamma!' She laughed.

'But Theo isn't a benefactor,' said Matt. 'He works in the school.'

'Oh no, Matt, don't be funny.'

'But he does,' said Matt. 'He says he's the odd job man. He even teaches the children sometimes, to learn poetry, he says. But mostly he does things like making up boilers and painting old furniture people give them.

'How does he do all that with one hand?' Caro said.

'He uses the funny one,' said Matt. 'It's only when he's

here that he doesn't, because Madame makes such a fuss. Don't you think it's beastly of her, Caro?'

'She's obviously got an obsession about it,' said Caro.

'What's that?' Matt asked.

'Well, it's letting something you don't like, or feel afraid of, get more and more important to you, so that in the end you can hardly think about anything else. Sometimes people go mad like that.'

'Is Madame going mad?' Matt said, doubtfully.

Caro laughed. 'No,' she said. 'Lots of people have kinks like that without going mad. Like hating cats, or snakes.'

'Well, poor Theo!' said Matt. 'He's not a cat or a snake.'

Caro only laughed, not taking it seriously.

But next time Theo was in the kitchen she asked a lot about the school, and Theo forgot to be shy and talked about it, and about Sam and Maggie, who had no children of their own and had decided to give up the rest of their lives to helping children in difficulties. He told them the stories of some of the children, too, and the ups and downs of the school, and how sometimes they had no money left to pay the bills and then suddenly someone they had never heard of would send them a cheque.

'St Raphael jogs their memories,' he said.

Caro said she wished she could have come and cooked for them, for nothing, but that she had always had to work for money because of Matt.

'We do pay our cook!' Theo said, smiling. 'And the cleaners. We would pay Miss Sonning too, if she would let us.'

'Who's Miss Sonning?' Matt asked.

'She's a retired schoolmistress who lives at St Raphael's

and is very good at teaching,' said Theo. 'She's nearly seventy.'

'It must be wonderful to be doing something like that,' said Caro. 'In spite of the difficulties, I'd love to help, but you see I'm going to be married soon.'

'Yes,' said Theo, going silent again, and not even congratulating her, so that Caro glanced at him in surprise.

But after this she talked to Theo more often than she had done before, even when Jasper was there. It was not really surprising, Matt thought, since Theo was much more interesting to talk to than Jasper, who was not keen on music or books or what was being done in the world, or any of the things Caro liked talking about. Caro and Theo seemed to have read a lot of the same things and though they didn't always agree about them, they seemed to like discussing their differences. They were both keen on poetry and Matt discovered it was Theo who had been trying to make into modern English verse the poem about the Phoenix which he had seen in the Library.

'But is it in German?' Matt said.

'No, in the sort of English that was spoken before the Norman Conquest,' said Theo. 'It's usually called Anglo-Saxon.'

'Did you learn that at school?' said Matt, surprised.

'No, I taught myself,' said Theo. 'I never could learn much at school. I like doing it better alone, at my own pace. I'll read some of the Phoenix to you, in Kennedy's version, and see if you don't like it very much.'

He read poetry just how Matt liked to hear it, fairly slowly, but without acting it, or moaning it.

The poem was about a paradisal place where, in a sacred grove, the unique Phoenix lived, and after a thousand years built its own funeral pyre and was burned to death, only to rise from the ashes, a new bird and yet the same. The Phoenix, Theo had explained first, was used to represent Christ, but he did not read all of the poem, only the beginning which told the story of the bird.

As Matt listened the wonderful grove with its fountain reminded him of the Rose Round, the flight of the Phoenix made him think of his imaginary journey south over desert and forest to the cold white pole, and when the sun was called a candle he remembered the words on the sundial on top of the tower: LUX UMBRA DEI. The sun was one of the stars, all candles burning away in heaven, and when they were gone the world would be at an end and time finished.

Theo read on, ending with the triumph of the Phoenix.

> Then all about him the race of birds
> In flocks assemble on every side,
> Hymning their hero in fervent strain:
> Around the Phoenix in circling flight
> They attend the holy one, high in air,
> Thronging in multitudes. Men look up,
> Marvel to see that happy host
> Worship the wild bird, flock after flock
> Keenly acclaiming and praising as king
> Their beloved lord; joyously leading
> Their liege to his home, till at last alone
> He swiftly soars where that blissful band
> May not follow after, when the best of birds
> From the turf of earth returns to his homeland.

Unfortunately Jasper came in just at the end. He clapped loudly.

'Consolation prize for reading: T. Ayre,' he said. 'But I hope you aren't going to favour us now with Casabianca, or A garden is a lovesome thing, God wot.'

'Oh shut up, Jasper,' said Caro quite crossly. 'Don't parade the fact that you've no ear for poetry.'

Jasper did not like that at all and turned sulky, and after this he started a new kind of teasing of Theo. He would make remarks like, 'Here comes your faithful swain, Caroline,' or 'Ask Cousin Theo to do it, he's longing for a chance to lick your boots', or 'Look at the dog-like devotion in his eyes.'

He spoke as if he meant to be funny, but Matt thought he was really trying to make Theo feel uncomfortable. In this he succeeded: Theo flushed easily and Jasper could see whenever he scored a hit, which at once roused him to further efforts. But his facetious remarks did not amuse Caro, and she once, in Matt's presence, told Jasper she wished he would not tease Theo about her.

'Well, don't encourage him then,' said Jasper. 'I don't like him always hanging about the place.'

'No more than you do,' said Caro.

'I happen to be engaged to you,' said Jasper, putting his arm round her waist.

'How is he to know that?' Caro said, shaking it off. 'Isn't it time you spoke to your father again? I'm tired of all this secrecy.'

'I wish you would leave me to manage Father my own way,' grumbled Jasper sulkily.

'I wish you'd get on with it, then,' said Caro, and they glared at each other across the kitchen table.

Matt began to wonder hopefully if the marriage might never take place. Caro had been engaged before and broken it off.

9

Exchange of Blows

On Caro's next day off she did not go out to meet Jasper. Instead she suggested that they should take their tea up to Bertrand's Tower, which she had not yet seen. Alix had got over her bad temper and was pleased to come too; so was Theo, who carried the picnic basket for Caro.

It was the end of August now, right at the end, and although it was a sunny day the air was indefinably clearer and sharper; summer was ending. As they walked up towards the tower Matt saw the signs on the sides of it and asked what they were.

'The signs of the zodiac,' said Theo. 'The months of the year.'

'Oh, so they are,' Matt said. 'There's the Bull sign, and there's the Ram. I didn't see them close enough before.'

Caro said, 'So Bertrand put pagan signs round his tower although he put the Benedicite over the door.'

'Well isn't that just like a seventeenth-century man?' said Theo. 'But Christians have always used the old wisdom of the pagans, look at the Phoenix. The sun symbols fit in particularly well, I always think. God must have thought so too, or Christ would not have died at Easter.'

'But Bertrand ended in La Trappe, Matt tells me,' said Caro. 'He gave up all his Natural Philosophy.'

'Not because it was wrong,' said Theo. 'Because he found that what he really wanted was supernatural philosophy.'

'Well, I wish he had married the lady he made the Rose Round for,' said Alix.

'She can't have loved him much if she married some-one else,' said Caro.

They went into the tower and showed Caro all over it. She was horrified by all the junk downstairs, so much so that her horror made Theo laugh.

'Clear it out? Why?' he said. 'Where should we put it all?'

'Throw it away, of course,' said Caro.

'Too much trouble,' said Theo. 'I used to spend half my time up here as a boy, but I didn't move it. I found useful things in it, from time to time. You never know what you mightn't find.'

'It would be a nice room without it,' said Caro.

'It's a nice room now,' said Theo.

Caro wrinkled her nose. 'Musty!' she said, laughing. 'How could you live in it like this?'

They went up the stairs, which Theo found rather a tight fit.

'Bertrand can't have been as big as you,' said Matt. 'Even if he did look like you.'

'Did he?' Caro said.

'Oh, people say so,' said Theo. 'He had a square face and black hair, but he wore rather a smart wig which improved his appearance.'

He went to a cupboard and got out a telescope which Matt had not seen before.

'We can't look at the stars by daylight,' he said. 'But we can look at the house.'

They climbed up the wooden ladder, which creaked under Theo's weight, making Alix giggle.

'Everything complains when you stand on it, Uncle Theo,' she said.

'Well, wouldn't you?' he said.

He fixed up the telescope stand in special slots for it on the parapet and they took it in turns to look through. It was quite a strong one: they could see every brick on the house, every rose in the Rose Round like this, from far away and above, a real bird's-eye view, a phoenix-eye view, Matt told himself, peering through the magnifying circles of glass.

'My turn, my turn,' Alix clamoured impatiently.

Matt resigned the telescope to her.

'I should like to see the stars through it,' he said.

'They're tiny,' said Alix. 'They look like hailstones.'

'You could look at the moon,' said Theo.

'Boo! I wouldn't like to come up the tower alone at night,' said Alix.

'Why not?' said Theo. 'I like it. The night is so still here, and you're right under the stars. I used to sleep up here sometimes and lie on my back, so that they were the last thing I saw.'

'If I lie on my back I get nightmares,' said Alix.

'Do you think people will really go to the moon?' said Matt.

'They had much better stay here,' said Theo. 'They don't know how to live on earth yet, let alone the moon.'

They went downstairs again. Theo and Caro went right outside, but Matt was attracted by the pile of junk which Theo had said he had never thoroughly explored. It would be so nice if there was something tremendously valuable there, which could be sold to provide a home for St Raphael's school. He began to ferret about, and Alix joined him. It was fascinating, though what they found was not at all valuable. Most of the things were broken. Theo had evidently added to the pile, for they found an old shoe which could only have belonged to him, and an exercise book with his name in and a lot of poems copied out in very bad handwriting.

Suddenly Matt gave a yell of dismay, which turned into a shriek of laughter.

'What is it?' Alix cried, climbing towards him.

'It's a foot! It's a foot!'

A white stone foot was sticking out in the excavation he had made in the rubbish. For just a moment Matt had thought it was real, and that there was a body under there.

'Murder in the summer-house!' Alix said, evidently thinking the same thing. 'Pull it out, Matt. Let's give Caro a fright.'

Matt gave the foot a pull. It did not move, but several other things did, and fell down on top of him.

'It's a statue,' said Alix. 'What fun! Let's unbury it.'

They worked away, lifting things off the buried statue and throwing them on to another corner of the junk-heap. Presently, all among the old chairs and broken tools and bounceless tennis balls, a marble lady lay, face down. They tried to lift her up, but she was much too heavy for them to move at all.

'Uncle Theo!' called Alix. 'Do come! We've found a statue.'

Theo was leaning against a pillar of the portico, talking to Caro, who had sat down on the lowest step, in the sun. He came in to look and Caro followed him.

'Turn her over,' Alix said.

'Easier said than done,' said Theo. But he got down in the hole Matt had made and managed to push his hand under the other side of the statue, and then he slowly levered her over.

'Why, it's Our Lady!' said Caro. 'Look at her rosary.'

'And I believe that bit under her foot is part of the moon,' said Alix.

'What's it made of?' Matt said. 'It's almost transparent, only not quite.'

'It's alabaster,' said Theo, carefully cleaning the carved face with his handkerchief.

'It's beautiful,' said Caro, gazing at it.

'Do stand it up, Uncle Theo,' said Alix.

'Isn't it too heavy?' Caro said.

'I'll try,' said Theo.

He had rather a struggle with the statue, but he got it upright in the end and stood it up against the wall, while Alix and Matt quickly pushed things under the pedestal to steady it, because it was broken and uneven underneath.

So there she stood, the alabaster Virgin, poised on the broken crescent of the moon, her hair and cloak swirling back in coils and folds, extravagant and decorative, her hands open and apart, her face smiling.

'I've never seen one quite like that,' said Caro. 'I like it.'

'I'd say it belonged to Bertrand's own time,' said Theo. 'How puzzling.'

'Oh!' cried Alix. 'I know where it comes from! It's the statue of the fountain!'

'But I thought you said your grandmother put the fountain in the garden,' said Matt.

'Yes, but Grandfather bought the statue abroad. It might have been an old one.'

'I believe you are right, Alix,' said Theo, slowly. 'But in that case, we must leave it here.'

'Oh, why?' Caro said. 'It would look lovely in its own place.'

'Because of Rosario, isn't it?' Matt said. 'Because she died.'

'Yes,' said Theo.

'Fancy, if Rosario were alive now she would be forty-five!' said Alix and began to laugh. 'What would Gran'mère feel about her then?'

'It's terribly wrong to refuse to accept her death, for all this time,' said Caro with a sigh.

There was a moment of silence while they looked at the lady posed in her invisible wind, full of grace, smiling.

Then Theo said, 'Well, what about having tea?'

So they went outside again and carried the picnic things round to the other side of the tower, where they were out of the wind and hidden from the house and full in the sun. From here they could look down over the brow of the ridge on the woods and the distant fields the other side, and they could see Severn, threading its silver ribbon through the heart of the land.

It gave Matt a sudden feeling of freedom to look out over the wide country: Woodhall, lost among the trees, ceased to be the whole world and was seen as only an island in it. Perhaps Caro felt this too, for she turned suddenly to Theo and said, 'Is this why you used to come up here, because from here you can see beyond Woodhall?'

Theo seemed surprised that she should say this, surprised perhaps that she had guessed so much of what he had felt.

'Yes,' he said. 'It's the same as looking at the stars: it takes you out of yourself.'

It was a very good place to picnic, and they settled down to enjoy it. Because they were behind the tower and looking away from the house they did not see Jasper till he came among them.

Jasper was in a very bad temper. He was angry because Caro had refused to go out with him, and angrier still to find out, from Agnes, that she was up here with the children and Theo. His way of being angry was not to shout and be done with it, but to pretend to be friendly and yet keep on making little digs, sharp remarks, unkind jokes, sneers. He very soon spoiled the picnic, reducing Theo to silence, Caro to frowns, and Matt to glowering. Only Alix, who was inclined to pick up a perverse mood when she sensed it, laughed at his jokes, and he encouraged her to join in his game. Most of it was teasing Theo, because teasing Caro was too dangerous, but Theo was easy to tease because he did not seem to know how to retaliate. Today it wasn't only his size and his stupidness Jasper was jeering at, but, what was much worse, his deformed arm, only he did it in an indirect, pretence-joking way that made it difficult to stop him without making Theo still more uncomfortable than he was.

Jasper seemed able to twist the conversation easily to his purpose.

Theo happened to answer a question of Matt's about Nero, saying that Price had taken him to the smith this afternoon to see about a loose shoe.

'You're lucky, Theo,' Jasper said. 'Whenever there's anything you don't want to do you can put your arm in a sling and wait for someone to do it for you.'

Alix giggled.

'I think I must try it,' said Jasper. 'So as not to have to do any work in the office. The glove's a good idea too, stops people asking questions.'

Alix, who was sitting next to Theo, suddenly said, 'What does it look like, Uncle Theo? Take your glove off.'

'No,' he said.

'Is it perfectly horrible?' said Alix hopefully.

'Alix!' said Caro.

Alix made a face. 'I want to see.'

'Don't be silly,' said Theo. 'Have another bun?'

He handed her the bag of buns and Alix, with a mischievous glint in her green eyes, caught hold of his arm, leant across, and pulled the glove off with her free hand.

Although he was shocked at her heartlessness Matt could not help looking at Theo's hand. As he had said, it was not like a proper hand. It was a small knobbly uneven thing with a sort of thumb and what looked like a couple of stumps of finger, growing in odd places. Matt felt a little sick in spite of himself.

There was an uncomfortable silence and then Jasper laughed.

Caro, who had been looking at Theo like everyone else, turned on Jasper. She said nothing, but her eyes were vivid with scorn.

Jasper laughed again, but uncomfortably.

'Well now, Alix,' said Theo quietly. 'Perhaps you'll give me back that glove, will you?'

Alix suddenly burst into tears.

'I wish I hadn't seen the horrid thing!' she cried. She jumped up, flung the glove down, and ran away into the wood crying.

'Oh dear,' Theo said unhappily, pushing his misshapen hand quickly out of sight in his pocket. 'Now she'll have nightmares.'

'Well, it will be her own fault,' said Caro. 'And perhaps teach her to think of other people's feelings sometimes.' She picked up the glove. 'Shall I put this on for you?'

Theo turned very red. 'No,' he said 'No, you mustn't do that.'

'What rubbish!' said Caro. She spoke firmly, but she took hold of his hand very gently.

The second time he saw it Matt did not feel at all sick. After all, it was only a piece of flesh and bone that had not grown the right shape. Caro put on the glove just as she used to put on Matt's gloves when he was too little to do it himself, in a neat businesslike way.

Jasper sat there staring at her in angry silence.

Suddenly he jumped up.

'Caroline, I want to talk to you.'

'I don't want to talk to you,' she said, coldly. 'In fact I'm going to look for Alix.'

'Then I'll come too.'

'No, you won't,' she said, so fiercely that Jasper did not follow her as she went away over the grass.

He turned and looked down at Theo, who was still sitting on the ground.

'Women!' he said. 'They love to have something to sentimentalize over.'

'What are you so angry about?' Theo said, looking up.

'Why do you think I'm angry?' Jasper said furiously. 'But she's not in love with you, she's just sorry for you.'

'I know that,' said Theo. 'Why should it matter to you?'

'Because she's in love with me,' Jasper said. 'She's promised to marry me.'

Theo gazed at him. 'Oh, it's you, is it?' he said at last. 'Well, I half-guessed that. So it's you who haven't the courage to marry her without your father's permission. What are you frightened of? Being cut off with a shilling?'

Jasper went quite pale with rage and Matt almost cheered.

'She doesn't seem afraid to earn her living, even if you are,' said Theo.

'I won't stand that kind of talk from you, Theo,' said Jasper.

'No, you like to do all the jeering yourself, don't you?' said Theo scornfully. 'Well, just for once you've put yourself in the wrong position.'

'Oh have I?' said Jasper. 'Well, I'm in the right position for putting you in your place, anyway.'

And without any warning he planted his foot against Theo's chest and kicked him backwards among the picnic things.

Theo scrambled to his feet, quickly for him, and advanced on Jasper with his fist clenched.

Jasper laughed. 'Surely you don't want to fight, Theo?' he said.

For answer Theo hit out at him and got in a blow that made Jasper stagger. Matt, excited, jumped to his feet. He saw that Jasper was now quite suddenly afraid of Theo, who, one-armed though he might be, was so tall and powerfully built and was now really roused, like a good-tempered bear who had been baited just too long. Jasper's fighting was all defensive and evasive, and in consequence not very effective. Theo punched him round the picnic things, crushing several plastic mugs and plates underfoot, and finally knocked him out on the chin. Jasper fell flat on the ground and lay there like a log, much to Matt's satisfaction.

But just then Caro and Alix came back out of the wood. Caro stared at the scene in astonishment. There was Theo, whom she had left sitting rather disconsolate and humiliated, standing with his hair on end, breathing hard and rubbing his sore knuckles on his trousers with a kind of surprised satisfaction. And there was Jasper on the ground, unconscious.

'Heavens!' cried Caro, astonished. She came running up and knelt down beside Jasper. 'What have you done to him?' she demanded accusingly of Theo.

'I knocked him down,' said Theo, still panting. 'He's all right. He'll come round in a moment.'

'You needn't have done that,' said Caro, lifting Jasper's head on to her knees. 'Oh look, he's terribly bruised. Poor Jasper.' With a change of mood more sudden than his own she looked up at Theo with blazing eyes. 'It was a brutal thing to do!'

Theo stepped backwards and on another picnic mug which crunched under his heel.

'I'm sorry,' he faltered. 'I got angry with him, I'm afraid.'

Alix was delighted with the signs of battle.

'Oh look at all the squashed mugs!' she cried hilariously.

Jasper groaned and opened his eyes. When he saw Caro bending over him so tenderly he murmured, 'Caro darling!' and gave a lop-sided smile of triumph.

Matt was annoyed. 'Jasper started it,' he said.

'You're no better than schoolboys,' said Caro, as if it was Theo who had made this excuse. 'I think we had better go home, Jasper. Can you get up? I'll help you.'

'I'll be all right in a moment,' he said, sitting up, and massaging his jaw. Caro's loving behaviour appeared to have restored his temper wonderfully. 'He took me by surprise.'

'What a lie!' muttered Matt.

Presently Jasper and Caro went off arm in arm down the ride. Neither of them said anything more to Theo.

'We'd better collect the things,' said Theo, gazing at the havoc he had made all round. 'What a mess!' he groaned. 'Oh dear, why did I have to do that? It was childish.'

'It was terrific!' said Matt with enthusiasm. 'Smashing!'

West Wind Blowing

THE next morning Matt happened to go out of the back door just as a man he had never seen before came in at the gate. He was a shortish, wiry man with ginger hair and a leathery face.

'Hullo,' he said cheerfully to Matt. 'You must be the Vision's brother.'

'What?' said Matt, astonished.

'We had a letter from Theo all about you and your sister,' said the man, his blue eyes twinkling. 'You won't know me. I'm a friend of Theo's, Sam Kingston.'

'I do know you, though,' said Matt triumphantly. 'You're the man who runs the school.'

'That's right,' said Sam Kingston. 'Maggie and I run it, with Theo's help. Mags is worried about old Theo. She thinks he's fallen badly for your sister. That's why I came instead of writing, thought I'd have a look round.' He stared up at the house and round about. 'Big place, this, isn't it? I knew Theo lived in a stately home, but I didn't realize how stately till I came up the drive. Tradesman's entrance for you, Sam, I said to myself. The butler won't let me in at the front.'

'There isn't a butler,' said Matt.

Just then Theo came out of the stables. He had been grooming Nero and was in his shirt-sleeves and not very clean.

'Sam!' he cried, delighted. 'How good to see you here.'

'I don't know if you'll repeat that when you hear why I've come,' Sam said.

'Why, what's happened?' Theo asked anxiously.

'Nothing terrible,' said Sam. 'Only Miss Sonning's sister is ill and she's gone to nurse her, and as you know Maggie and I had planned to go to this conference. We don't feel dear old Mrs Bush is quite the person to leave in sole charge of the Number Ones. Mags says she'll give up the conference, but I don't want her to, if you can possibly come back.'

'Of course I'll come,' said Theo. 'I'm not doing anything here.'

'What, no huntin', shootin' and fishin' going on?' Sam teased him. 'You smell pretty horsy all the same.'

'Well, naturally, since I've just been in the stable,' said Theo. 'Come along, Sam. We'll see if Miss Rendal can manage some lunch for you, and we'll catch a train this afternoon.'

They went into the kitchen. Caro shook hands, as interested as Matt had been to meet Mr Kingston. Sam gave her a keen glance and then smiled.

'Who are the Number Ones you're going to take charge of, Theo?' Matt asked.

'The children who have no homes to go to in the holidays,' he said. 'Sam, I'm afraid this will sound peculiar but would you mind having lunch in the kitchen?'

'I'd be honoured,' said Sam, with a bow to Caro. 'Behind the green baize door for me every time! Did you know my grandfather was head groom in a ducal establishment? Well, he was, so you can see this is my proper place.'

'I wish it was mine too,' said Theo. 'But if I am going away I must have lunch with Mamma, and I don't want you to, because I know she will be intolerably rude to you and I couldn't stand that.'

When he had gone to wash and change Sam said, 'I'd like to have seen the Wicked Stepmother all the same.'

'She's his real mother,' said Matt.

'She doesn't behave like one, does she?' said Sam. 'Mags and I call her that because she sounds such an impossible old tyrant, not to say downright cruel where Theo is concerned. When we first met him, years ago now, he couldn't bear to let anyone see that arm of his, it was all done up in a sling.'

'He has to wear a sling here, when he's with Madame,' said Matt.

'Madame? Good name for her,' said Sam. 'As far as we could see she not only never let him use it, so that it was much weaker than it need have been, but made him feel he was a kind of monster sent to make her life unendurable, not to say the cause of his little sister's death, or some nonsense. It took us ages to put some fight into him. Even now he's much too meek.'

'He isn't always,' said Caro suddenly, and from the way she shut her mouth Matt knew she was still annoyed with Theo for knocking Jasper down the day before.

Sam gave her a quick look. 'Glad to hear it,' he said.

'You can have a squint at Madame through the hatch,' Matt told him and Sam at once availed himself of this invitation.

'Hm, she's certainly *formidable*,' he said, pronouncing it the French way, with a wry grin, as he came back. 'It's a marble face, isn't it? A mask, and yet there's lots of energy stored up there, yeasting inside, only coming out as hatred. Poor thing.'

Matt was surprised at that 'Poor thing'.

'That elf-faced child is Theo's niece, I suppose?' Sam went on. 'The daughter of the Welsh siren who broke his youthful heart by marrying his all-conquering brother.'

'Did she?' said Caro. 'I wondered whether that had happened when he spoke about her, once.'

'Oh, he got over that long ago,' said Sam. 'But Theo's got the most breakable heart of anyone I know. Unfortunately he always seems to choose to fling it at the feet of people who have no use for it.'

He looked hard at Caro. She said nothing, but she turned rather red and went to take the puddings out of the oven.

After lunch, since Madame was safely in her room, resting, Theo took Sam round part of the house, and told Matt he could come too. Matt felt terribly guilty once he was out of the back regions, in spite of the fact that he was with the real owner of the house. But it was so much more interesting going round with Theo than being hurried through by impatient Alix, that presently he almost forgot Madame's distant, forbidding presence.

They went into the Library, and now Matt was able to see the famous portrait of Bertrand, which hung over one of the marble fireplaces. There he was in his black curled wig, wearing a smart plum-coloured coat and a great many ruffles of elegant lace, with a sword at his side and a ridiculous little dog at his feet, and he stood with his hand on the celestial globe that was now in the tower on the ridge. He did look a little like Theo, but his face was much harder and more determined, and he looked as if his conversation would be witty and keen-edged, and as if his sword was no mere ornament to his costume.

'I can't imagine him a Trappist,' Matt said.

'I can,' said Theo. 'Put a cowl instead of a wig and he looks rather like a Dominican father I know.'

Sam said, 'What a lot of interesting stuff you've got here, Theo. I can't imagine living in a house like this. Is it open to the public?'

'Good gracious no,' said Theo. 'There isn't really much here that collectors would notice. All the same, I'd sell most of it, if Mamma would allow it, and St Raphael's could have the proceeds. But she won't, of course.'

As they went upstairs Matt said, 'Which rooms would you have let the school have, Theo?'

'What's this?' said Sam at once.

Evidently Madame had been quite wrong, for Sam knew nothing of Theo's plan. But now the subject had come up it was talked of a good deal.

'My dear Theo, it was a wonderful idea,' Sam said regretfully. 'What a pity your mother won't hear of it! Though, I must say, I understand her point of view. It would be difficult to keep the children entirely out of sight and hearing.'

Presently they went up to Theo's own room. It was at the same level as Matt's, two floors up, but it looked over the lawn. Theo hastily began to pack a suitcase for himself; Caro would have been shocked at the muddle of it. Matt looked round. It was a bare room, he thought, except that there were a lot of books in it. The curtains and carpet and counterpane were all faded and worn. The crucifix on the wall was carved out of wood.

'I like that,' said Sam, standing in front of it. 'Is it Austrian?'

'In a way,' said Theo. 'It was made by a prisoner of war, but the wood is English. The first war, I mean: it belonged to my father. I found it in a trunk, when I was a boy. Price told me where it came from.'

He shut his suitcase and they all went downstairs through the great silent empty house. Caro was not in the kitchen.

Theo looked all round, disappointed.

'Will you say good-bye to Caro for me, Matt?' he said. 'I hope you'll both be here at Christmas.'

'Unless Jasper marries her before then,' said Matt gloomily.

'Don't let him,' said Theo with a smile, not a very happy one.

'What's all this?' Sam asked.

'I'll tell you on the way home,' said Theo.

'But this is your home, Theo,' said Matt.

'St Raphael's feels more like home to me,' he said. 'Good-bye, Matt. Write to me sometimes, if you feel like it.'

He shook Matt by the hand and picked up his suitcase. Matt stood and watched them go out of the yard gates and suddenly felt sorry Theo had gone and almost lost without him. He looked up at the house and saw Caro at her window.

'Theo's gone,' he said.

'Yes, I can see them walking down the drive,' said Caro.

Both of them were rather silent that evening. Once Matt sighed.

'What is it, Matty?'

'I wish Theo hadn't gone.'

She said nothing and Matt said. 'Aren't you sorry he's gone?'

'Well, I had got used to having him about,' Caro

admitted. 'However, perhaps Jasper will be happier now he's not here.'

But Jasper, when he came, said he had to get back to his office in Birmingham. The bruise on his chin revived Caro's indignation with Theo for his brutal attack, as she called it, much to Jasper's delight. He spent some time walking about with her in the shrubberies, and kissing her, but when she came in Matt did not think she looked very happy.

'I don't believe you really like Jasper, Caro,' he said, when Jasper had gone.

'Don't be silly, Matt,' she said, quite sharply. 'Of course I like him. It will be lovely when we can be married and have our own place at last, won't it?'

She always spoke as if Matt were marrying Jasper too.

Everyone was going away and summer was going too. It was September now, and days were not so long, the night came sooner and was colder. It would soon be time to go back to school and Aunt Maud in Birmingham. Alix was mournful.

'It will be dull without you, Matt,' she said.

Although she so often teased him and irritated him Matt really quite liked her. She was an odd creature, but it was never boring to do things with her. They sat in their tree house, which was finished at last, and Alix said, 'Vow and promise to come back, Matt.'

'Don't be silly,' said Matt. 'Of course I'll come back for next holidays, perhaps even at half-term.'

'So long as Caro doesn't go and marry the man she's engaged to,' said Alix. 'Whose name begins with J.'

'Alix! How do you know?'

'Guess!' Alix said, laughing. 'The day Uncle Theo knocked him down I was sure. Still, even if she marries

Jasper you could come, because then we should be relations. Cousins-in-law, or something. Vow and promise.'

'Oh, all right.'

It was silly, but it pleased Alix, and Matt was a little flattered to feel she cared as much as that. She gave him a lucky pig, so he had to give her his old silver threepenny bit with a hole in it, although he would rather have kept that than have the pig.

Alix immediately put it on the chain with the medal she wore round her neck.

Before he left for school Matt went into the wood alone and through the old blue door, and on into the rose garden, looking through the yew hedge first to make sure no one was there.

No, there was no one there, and the air was cool, the grass damp with recent rain. Matt went slowly towards the circle; the roses were beginning to bloom again after their August rest. He stood with his back to the fountain and looked through the western arch at the sun setting, hidden behind long clouds that glowed like fires and like wings of flame. The Phoenix, he thought, imagining the great pyre, the glowing feathers, and the immortal bird immolating itself, golden like the sun.

He walked a little way towards the western arch; the yellow roses were pale in the shadowy air. A small wind was blowing out of the west against his face, a wet wind that he felt might grow to a great gale and roar through the forests outside the garden. The wind came over the mountains of Wales and the mountains of Ireland, those ancient countries, homes of harp and song and sad tales of loss and wandering; the wind came from the sea, the great grey Atlantic, the huge tides, thousands of miles across where no land was, only the waste of water, the mystery of chaos and the deep. And what then? America, the fabulous continent, once the new lands, always the strange lands, full of marvels. And miles and miles farther, the other ocean, deepest, widest on earth, the vast Pacific.

Matt stood there dreaming of those far-off seas, the legends of those lands, the prize and grave of all who go out to look for what they have not got, and a little rain began to fall, like a mist on his face, and the sun sank lower, shadow rose round him, the clouds faded to embers.

He turned round, and just for the flash of an instant he thought he saw by the fountain the face of a man, winged, and it was like his own face, but ancient.

'Matthew!' he whispered aloud, feeling he was naming not only himself.

But there was only water there, leaping up from the narrow circle of jets, falling in a continual shower round the broken pedestal where once the statue had been. The Lady was not in her garden, there was no centre to the ring of roses.

And now it really began to rain and night was coming, Matt ran away, back to the kitchen, the firelight, the warmth of the hearth.

11

Dark November

In Birmingham it rained and rained and term began, and a new school year. Matt was in a new form, so was Tunstall. Tunstall had a lot of new matchboxes from Wales, Matt had none. They played football and did lessons and it was not summer any more but winter, and Woodhall seemed far away, a place on the other side of the world.

In October Matt got a letter from Theo. Theo's left-handed writing was much worse than Matt's right-handed writing, in spite of the difference in their ages. Theo asked when Matt's half-term was, and if he would like to go down to Woodhall with him. Of course Matt said yes, and Theo came on Friday at lunch-time to fetch him from Aunt Maud's house.

Aunt Maud was alarmed by Theo. He was so very big he made her drawing-room look like a dolls' house, and it was so full of treasures she was sure he would knock something over. So was he, and one small table did go flying, but there was nothing on it and it was not damaged. But Theo breathed a sigh of relief when he was safely in the road again, and Matt could give free vent to his laughter.

'Talk about bulls in china shops!' he said.

It was the beginning of November, just after All Saints' and All Souls', bonfire time, firework time and the season of fog when the dark begins to close in early. Woodhall stood bleak among stark leafless trees, and it was cold. The great rooms, empty and unheated, held the cold. Madame's rooms, Mademoiselle's, Alix's, these had fires lit in them, but the rest of the house was like the halls of the Snow Queen's palace, except for the kitchen, which was always warm.

Alix came running through the green-baize door to greet Matt, full of delight. Caro was smiling and cheerful. Everything seemed all right.

And yet that November visit did not go very well. Madame had a touch of lumbago and the ache in her back seemed to provoke an ache in her temper. She commanded Theo's presence much more often than usual, mainly because she wanted help to rise from her chair. But if he ever offered help of his own accord she at once became unreasonably angry. Once Matt, peeping through the hatch, saw this happen.

Madame was trying to get up from her place. She had her stick in her hand, but her first effort was unsuccessful and she sat back in her chair with a grimace of impatience.

'Shall I help you, Mamma?' Theo said, going up to her with his hand out ready.

'I do not need your help, imbécile!' cried Madame, her eyes beady with fury. 'I am not yet on my way to the grave, much as you would like that!' And she struck his arm out of the way with her cane.

Yet she could not rise alone and had to call Alix to help her. She was imperious with Alix, as with everyone else, but she encouraged Alix's own imperious quality. Alix did not like having to dance attendance on her grandmother while Matt was at Woodhall, and that made her irritable. She did not dare to contradict Madame, and so she let off the worst of her temper at Theo, because she knew very well she would not be reprimanded whatever she said to him. Theo got the worst of it all round. Nothing he could do was right, and perhaps because of this he seemed more clumsy than usual, calling down more wrath on himself by knocking things over and sitting on the wrong chairs and cracking them, and provoking tirades at every meal by fumbling ineffectively with his food, so that quite often he hardly ate anything at all and used to take pieces of brown bread out of the kitchen when he thought no one was looking.

It rained and rained, and Matt and Alix could not go out in the woods, and it was cold in the sheds. They had to spend most of their time in the kitchen, and that was dull, and Agnes was always there, and in the mornings Mrs Monkleigh from the village as well, coming in and out with her cleaning things.

Caro was not in a very good mood either, Matt discovered. Jasper had not come since the summer, and had not written very often either, and he had not got any further with his father, so that Caro was not pleased. But that did not seem to make her more friendly to Theo. She seemed impatient with him, always trying to get him out of the way, Matt thought. He saw that Theo was having a miserable week-end and that added to his own disappointment.

The climax came on Monday, the last day of the holiday. Sir Godfrey and Lady Hartnoll and Freda were coming to lunch and Caro was very busy and rather hurried because the food was not the kind that could be prepared the day before. Madame was very particular as to what Sir Godfrey had to eat; so was Sir Godfrey. Caro was not in the best of tempers and when Theo came in from the scullery carrying a dusty bottle of wine she said sharply, 'I'm afraid I haven't any time for coffee this morning.'

'I don't want any coffee,' Theo said. 'But I do want to ask you something rather important.'

'Oh, for heaven's sake, what a time to choose!' said Caro, crossly. 'Do get out of the way.' She pushed past him impatiently and he stepped back hastily, knocked his elbow on the dresser and dropped the bottle of wine. It smashed into a hundred pieces, wine flooded over the floor and its pungent smell filled the room.

'Oh!' cried Caro in rage and despair. 'Now look what you've done! I'll never get this wretched meal ready in time.'

'I'll clear it up,' said Theo anxiously, squatting down and beginning to collect the broken glass.

'Matt,' said Caro. 'Get him a dustpan, for goodness' sake.'

Matt brought the dustpan and saw Theo had cut his fingers on the glass. It was not surprising, because his hand was shaking. They swept up the glass and Theo got a floorcloth and tried to clean up the floor.

'Oh, that'll do,' said Caro at last. 'I'd rather have you out of the way.'

Theo took the cloth into the scullery to wash it out under the tap, but every time he squeezed it out blood soaked into it from his cut fingers.

'Let me do it,' said Matt.

Theo gave him the cloth and wound up his hand in his handkerchief.

'Matt, could you come down to the cellar with me and carry up the wine?' he said. 'I don't want to drop it again.'

The cellar stairs were behind a door in the scullery and were steep and narrow, plunging into darkness. Theo switched on the light, but it was not very bright. Following him down, Matt found himself in a huge musty cavern, full of cobwebs, dust lying thick everywhere. Arches in the farther wall seemed to lead away into other cellars.

'It's a labyrinth down here,' Theo said. 'There's only light in this one, and I had that put in. It was candles when I was a boy.'

He went and peered at the wine bottles in their racks.

'Father put down most of these,' he said. 'Uncle Godfrey tells me what to get now. After all, he's the one who drinks it, usually.'

Matt peered through the dark arches.

'Hoo! Hoo!!' he called, and heard a faint echo. 'Hooooo!'

'I shouldn't like to be down here by myself,' he said. 'Not if the light went out.'

'I was, once,' said Theo.

'When you were grown up?'

'No, when I was a good deal smaller than you,' said Theo. 'There's another way in to these cellars, which is never used. Julian once pushed me in and bolted the door on me.'

'But wasn't he younger than you? Couldn't you have fought him?' Matt said, surprised.

Theo said, 'Well, he had two friends staying at the time. Julian was a great one for gang action. It was supposed to be a joke, like most of his efforts, but it was no joke to me. No light! I couldn't see anything, and they went off and left me there, and then I couldn't hear anything either. It was like a nightmare, except that nothing happened. It was just dark and huge and silent and cold; like being in a cave underneath the earth.'

'What did you do?' Matt asked.

'Shook with fright,' said Theo, smiling.

'Yes, but to get out. Did you bang on the door?'

'I couldn't reach it. You see, it was a trap-door.'

'How awful!' said Matt. It was easy to imagine the horror of it, down here in the dim wine cellar.

'I didn't dare move for fear of getting lost,' said Theo. 'So I just sat on the floor for hours and hours. Julian and the gang had gone out to tea and forgotten me. Of course it seemed much longer than it was. Then I heard someone a long way off in another cellar and I shouted, and it was Price, and he came along with a candle and found me.'

It seemed funny to think of Price there when Theo was only a little boy. It all seemed years ago to Matt; long before he was born this had happened to Theo, being shut in the dark cellar by his careless young brother.

'Theo,' he said, 'why is Price so silent always?'

'He's just like that,' said Theo. 'He distrusts people. He's had a lot of bad luck with them in his life. But he's good himself, completely trustworthy, though it's probably never occurred to him that he knows at least one person like that, himself!' He added, 'Price has always been good to me.'

He had found the bottle he wanted.

'Matt,' he said, 'why is Caro so angry with me?'

'She's just in a hurry today,' said Matt.

'No, it's not only that,' said Theo and he sighed. 'Well, never mind. But I wanted to ask her something important.'

'What?' Matt asked.

'Well, we've got to leave our house in December, the school I mean, and I've promised to look after three of the children in the holidays. If Caro would agree, I would bring them here, and keep them this side of the house.'

'I'm sure she would agree,' Matt said.

'Well, look here, could you ask her? Because I must tell Mamma at lunch-time, it's the last chance I shall have.'

'Why don't you write?'

'She hates letters. Besides, I'd rather get it over.'

'Suppose she says no?' Matt said.

'She will, I expect,' said Theo. 'But I think I shall have to do it whatever she says.'

They climbed up the cellar steps and Theo went off to change his clothes.

Caro had now got her cooking under control and was a little calmer. Matt picked his moment and then told her what Theo had said.

Caro stared at him, red in the face.

'Is that what he wanted?' she said, and looked as if she were going to cry. 'And I was so cross with him!'

'You would help with those children, wouldn't you?' said Matt.

'Of course I would, I'd love to help,' said Caro. 'But how can I let him know?'

'I'll tell him,' said Matt, and ran off upstairs. He knew how to get to Theo's room now from their own. It was only a question of going along a passage, up a couple of steps and through a door which was supposed to shut off the servants' quarters, but which was now never locked. Theo used what had once obviously been the nursery bathroom and he was in it now, Matt saw, as the door was open. He was half-dressed, looking rather smarter than usual in a new shirt, and he was trying to put sticking plaster on his fingers and getting very stuck up with it. Matt had not realized before what a lot of ordinary things become difficult if you have only got one hand to do them with.

Theo looked up at the sound of his feet. 'Just in time, Matt,' he said, holding out his hand with a smile.

Matt plastered the cuts and told him what Caro had said. Theo seemed very relieved.

'She was sorry about being cross, too,' said Matt.

'Was she?'

'Yes, almost crying,' said Matt. 'She isn't a cross person really.'

'I'm sure she isn't,' said Theo.

He put on the jacket of his suit and Matt said, 'You do look smart today, Theo!'

Theo laughed and said, 'It's only because Uncle Godfrey will be there. He won't like what I'm going to say, and so I'm not going to give him a chance to make his usual remarks about my looking like a tramp, not to mention behaving like one.'

'It sounds quite like a battle,' said Matt.

'It is, for me,' said Theo.

They went down the back stairs and he looked in at the kitchen door. Agnes was there, so he only said, questioningly, 'All right, Caro?'

'Oh yes, Theo,' she said, in quite a different voice, not cross, rather pleading and humble.

Theo smiled and went away.

'Really, he can look quite tidy when he wants to,' said Caro. 'I've never seen him look so smart! You can believe he's the owner of this house when he looks like that. What's come over him, I wonder?'

Matt told her what Theo was going to do, and that he had said it was like a battle for him.

Caro laughed. 'If Madame says no, he'll give in,' she said.

Matt, doing his job at the hatch again, was determined

not to miss what was going on. He was careful to remind Agnes to bring him Theo's plate, so that he could cut everything up for him, and when he was doing it he caught Theo's eyes, and got a smile from him, a conspirator's smile.

When Theo announced his intention of bringing the three children for Christmas Madame began by saying 'Certainly not,' as if that disposed of the subject.

'I'm afraid I am bringing them, Mamma,' said Theo. 'I won't allow them to disturb you. I shall look after them myself, and Miss Rendal is willing to do the extra cooking.'

Madame was so astonished that he should not obey her, that she had nothing to say for the moment. Sir Godfrey however, had plenty.

He gave Theo a prolonged lecture, saying the same thing over and over in slightly different and more angry ways, which was that he had no consideration for his mother and that the Kingstons were making use of him for their own ends.

Theo defended Sam and Maggie, but otherwise he did not say very much. Freda went on eating steadily and only paused to say once, 'I can't think why you're making such a fuss about these children, Theo. After all, you're not a teacher or a social worker. Why can't you leave them alone?'

Theo said nothing to this either.

Every time Matt came to the hatch Theo was being lectured and argued at. He did not get very much to eat because Madame curtly ordered the plates to be removed as soon as the others had finished.

'Mr Ayre has finished,' she said firmly to the hesitant Agnes, although it was quite plain he had not.

Theo gave up his plate, but stuck to his point.

'I've promised,' he said. 'I think the children must come first; it's for Christmas.'

Madame was very angry.

'You are doing it to spite me, Théodore,' she said in her sharpest, coldest voice.

'No, Mamma.'

'Trying to show me you are master of the house,' said Madame.

Theo said nothing.

But when they rose from luncheon he had not given in. Matt ran out to tell Caro.

'Good for him,' she said, smiling.

When Theo came out to collect Matt and say good-bye she was smiling and friendly to him, and made him take some sandwiches she had made.

'Matt said you didn't have time to eat much,' she said. 'I'm glad the children are coming.'

'It's very kind of you to say you'll help,' said Theo.

Alix was there too, to say good-bye, and she gave Matt a matchbox.

'What's this for?'

'Your collection,' she said.

'But I've got lots of "England's Glory".'

Alix's face fell and Matt said hastily, 'Oh, there's a new joke on the back. That will be useful.'

Alix cheered up and she and Caro stood in the back door and waved as Theo and Matt went off into the murky, rainy afternoon.

12

Dangerous Christmas

THEO wrote to Matt and told him a little about the three children he was bringing to Woodhall and gave the time of the train in Birmingham so that Matt could meet him and travel with him if he wanted to.

'It would be a help to have you,' he wrote.

When Matt arrived at the station he soon saw Theo and his charges. There was one boy in a wheelchair; he looked about ten, with a lively mischievous face. The girl looked older; she had an artificial arm. The smallest boy was wrapped up in a rug and Theo was carrying him.

'Here's Matt,' said Theo and introduced them. The girl was called Bernadette and the boy in the chair was Mickey.

'And this is Noel,' Theo said, 'who's going to have double presents because he was lucky enough to be born on Christmas Day.'

'Unlucky enough,' said Mickey. 'I bet he only gets one present.'

Noel's small peaky face peered out of the rug at Matt, but he said nothing.

Sam Kingston came down the platform, carrying sweets and comics which he handed to Bernadette. When the train came in there was a reserved carriage for them, and together Sam and Theo and Matt got the children in, and Mickey's wheelchair. Mickey's legs were deformed from an accident he had had as a small child, as Matt knew from Theo's letter. When they were settled Sam got out again and shut the door.

. . . he soon saw Theo and his charges.

'Good luck, Theo!' he called out, as the train moved off.

'Why did he say, "Good luck"?' Mickey asked.

'Thought I'd need it with all of you to look after,' said Theo, smiling. 'Still, Matt's come to keep you in order.'

Mickey looked doubtfully at Matt, who grinned, so then Mickey laughed and bagged his comic from Bernadette.

Theo had put Noel down on the seat, with his head on his lap, and he kept his hand over him all the time, in case the train should jerk badly and shift him.

Mickey and Bernadette read their comics from end to end and then began to chatter and look out of the window, or sometimes at Matt, not quite sure of him yet, but Noel said nothing, only gazed at the ceiling. He seemed very feeble, but not exactly ill.

Price met them with the old brake and helped to get them all safely stowed away. It was a fine December day, but not very warm, and there were plenty of rugs in the car. When they reached Woodhall Caro ran out into the yard to help unpack everybody. She was wearing a bright red sweater and a black skirt and looked very gay and cheerful. She guessed all the children's names right and she had a wonderful tea ready for them in the kitchen, with a sugar mouse sitting on each plate. The mouse was a great success with Noel and when Theo carried him off to bed, he was clutching it, still uneaten, in his hand.

'Shall I put him to bed, Theo?' Caro asked.

'I will tonight,' said Theo. 'He's used to me.'

They all went upstairs to see their rooms. Theo had to put Noel down on his bed to go and fetch Mickey. The boys were to share the room next to Theo's. Bernadette's was farther away, near where Caro and Matt slept, in the old maids' bedrooms. Bernadette was astonished and delighted to find flowers in her room, white Christmas roses.

Theo gave Noel a bath in his bathroom and when Matt went in to give him a towel he had called for, he saw skinny little Noel, supported by Theo's arm like a baby, feebly splashing with his feet and grinning, and Theo was encouraging the splashing. Alix peeped round the door while the little boy was being dried on Theo's knee.

'I've brought Noel my rabbit to go to bed with,' she said. 'He's rather old, but nice, I think.'

Noel solemnly took the battered velvet rabbit.

'Say thank you to Alix,' said Theo.

'Thank you, Alix,' Noel repeated. After that he suddenly became quite talkative. All the time Theo was drying him and putting on his pyjamas he talked away about all sorts of people and things, belonging to the school, Theo told them.

Everybody came in to see Noel go to bed. Theo held him up in front of the crucifix to say his prayers. At the end of them he said, 'Holy Archangel Raphael, protect us all.'

'We always say that,' said Theo, putting Noel in bed and kissing him. 'Now, go to sleep, Noel. Mickey will be in bed very soon.'

'Kiss Alix,' said Noel.

Alix was rather flattered, and came over and kissed him.

'Kiss Caro,' said Noel.

Caro laughed and kissed him. 'Good night, you baby.'

'He plays baby too much,' said Theo.

'Kiss Matt,' said Noel hopefully.

'He's just putting off the evil hour of good-night,' said Theo. 'No more kissing, Noel. Bed now.'

He collected Mickey and turned off the light.

'How old is Noel?' Alix asked when they were outside.

'He's seven,' said Theo, 'but he's had such a lonely miserable life so far he's more babyish than he ought to be. He's got something wrong with his bones and his back, he can't move by himself and his wretched relations used to leave him for hours alone in the house.'

'Were they Catholics?' Matt asked.

'Yes, not very good ones,' said Theo. 'They were poor and they thought Noel was just a nuisance. His mother died when he was born, and they don't know who his father was. I'm afraid we spoil him rather.'

He went to bath Mickey and the others went downstairs to clear up the tea and get the supper. Bernadette, in spite of her artificial hand, was quite useful.

'I always help Mrs Kingston,' she said proudly.

'You're very good at using your hand,' said Matt.

'Oh, it was difficult at first, I couldn't do a thing with it,' said Bernadette. 'But now I always say it's much more use than Theo's hand and he'd better get one too!'

Carefully drying a saucer she remarked, 'What a big house, isn't it? Fancy us coming to a grand place like this. It's like something on the pictures.'

Later, when she too was in bed, Theo, who had been away to see his mother, came back into the kitchen.

'Thank you both very much,' he said. 'The children all feel quite at home now.'

'Thank you for bringing them, Theo,' said Caro seriously. 'It's just right for Christmas.'

Christmas, of course, did not come straight away, and there seemed to be a great deal to do before it came, with several expeditions to Bewdley and one to Kidderminster, to buy presents and things to make presents. Although Caro had a lot more to do she seemed happy about it, and whistled and sang as she worked. Bernadette helped, and she knew all the latest songs, for she was a great film fan, and a wireless fan too. Caro's songs were usually old ones, ballads and so on.

Alix and Matt found time to go and look at their house in the tree. It looked very obvious now that there were no leaves to hide it in secrecy, but it was still fairly solid.

'It's like an enormous nest,' said Alix. 'Made by ostriches.'

Matt's pleasure was a little spoiled by Jasper's arrival at his father's house for Christmas, because of course he often came over to Woodhall to see Caro. Jasper was more cautious about teasing Theo since the day of the picnic, and anyway Theo was so busy looking after Noel and Mickey that he did not have much time for anything else.

'Jasper's going to have it out with Sir Godfrey this time,' Caro told Matt.

'I was hoping you had decided not to marry Jasper,' said Matt, disappointed.

'My dear Matt! Why?'

'Because I don't like him.'

'Oh Matt, don't be silly.'

'It's not silly. He's an unkind person. He's horrid to Theo.'

'Well, I like that!' cried Caro. 'When Theo attacked him in that extraordinary way, quite unlike himself, too.'

Matt saw it was no good arguing.

On the afternoon of Christmas Eve there was a great hurrying and scurrying. Caro was cooking for the next day and the children were doing up presents and decorating the kitchen and Caro's sitting-room with holly and ivy and home-made paper chains. Matt went out with Theo to cut a fir tree, out of the warm busy house into the wide bare woodland, misty, darkening already, cold, silent, still. Even the pines were silent, standing up like shadows in the windless air.

It was a small pine they cut in the end, not a fir. Its blue-green stiff boughs opened flat from the stem like fans, in three separate rings, a small one on top like the spikes of a crown, with a wider circle a foot or so down, and beneath that a larger spread still of the sweet-smelling needles.

'I like it to be a pine,' Matt said.

Their voices sounded in the still air as they went home, Theo carrying the tree and Matt pulling long streamers of ivy from the trees as he went by.

They put the cut tree in a tub and carried it into the kitchen to be decorated. Everyone wanted to do it.

'Someone must stay with Noel,' Theo said.

Noel was on the sofa in the sitting-room, by the fire, among all the presents and holly and paper chains. Bernadette had just been with him, but had come in to see the tree.

'Shall I, Theo?' she said, looking at the decorations wistfully.

'Alix will go and read to him, won't you Alix?' said Theo.

'All right,' said Alix, reluctantly.

'We'll leave the star for you to put on the top of the tree,' said Theo.

'And some of the other things? A bell? One of the birds?'

'Yes.'

Alix went off, rather slowly.

'Is that fair?' Caro said.

'I think it's good for Alix,' said Theo. 'She never has to do things for other people.'

They were all very busy. Matt helped Mickey to hang some things on the lower boughs of the tree. Bernadette wound tinsel round the stem. Caro was busy clearing up her cooking things and Theo was fetching logs from the shed in a big basket.

Suddenly Mickey said, 'Coo! There isn't half a smell of burning! Caro's burnt the mince pies.'

'I haven't,' she said. 'There's nothing in the oven now.'

She opened the door and they all saw smoke in the passage.

'Oh, Theo!' cried Caro, with a gasp of alarm.

Theo dumped his log basket and ran through into the passage, the others ran after him, Mickey pushing his wheel-chair along at a great pace.

Alix was coming down the back stairs as Theo opened the sitting-room door. She gave a great shriek.

'Oh! Noel! Oh!'

The sitting-room was full of smoke and flames seemed to be leaping up everywhere. The paper chains and present boxes were flaring up and there was a dreadful smell of singeing. Noel's sofa was in the middle of all the burning things.

Theo ran into the room, caught up Noel and brought him out, putting him in Caro's arms.

'What is it? What is it?' he was saying sleepily.

Theo went back into the room and began trampling on the burning paper chains. He seized a rug from the sofa and threw it over the pile of burning presents.

'Oh, my dolly I made!' wailed Bernadette.

The doll was lying in a pyre of burning cardboard. Theo grabbed at her, grabbed again and got her. He rolled her up in the edge of the rug and then stuffed her into his pocket.

'Get some water, Matt,' he said. 'The carpet's smouldering.'

Alix cried, 'Oh! Is the house going to burn down?'

'Of course not,' said Theo. 'Get some water.' He was kicking the embers of a log back into the fire-place.

Matt and Alix rushed to the scullery and came staggering back with full buckets of water.

'Steady! Don't drown the place,' Theo said.

He was stamping out the paper and anything else that was burning. Now there were no flames left, only smoke and a smell of scorching.

Matt and Alix slopped water about and got rather wet about the feet.

Presently there was nothing alight but the fire. Theo put the guard in front of it. The room was in a dreadful mess.

'Oh dear,' said Caro, gazing round.

'It's all my fault,' Alix said, crying dismally. 'Noel went to sleep and I got bored and I went to get a book and then I started reading it upstairs and I forgot all about Noel and he might have been burnt to death.'

'Well, I daresay you won't do it again,' Theo said. 'Not that I'll trust you with Noel any more.'

Alix wailed louder than ever.

'I'm sorry! I'm terribly sorry!' she howled.

'So you should be,' said Theo.

'Oh! Oh! Oh!' sobbed Alix desolately.

Caro said, 'Alix, dear, I'm sure you'll be very careful next time you're left in charge of anyone. Come along to the kitchen all of you. Is it all right here, Theo?'

'Yes, I think so.'

They all went back to the kitchen, Alix still sniffing and gasping.

'But what happened?' Matt said. 'How did it start, the fire?'

'A log fell out of the fire and set light to all that paper,' said Theo. 'Lucky you smelt it so soon, Mick.'

Caro put Noel down on the old horsehair settee in the kitchen.

'I wasn't burnt at all, I wasn't,' he said triumphantly.

Theo sat down on one of the wooden chairs. It creaked, but he went on sitting in it.

'Oh Theo, you've burnt your hand,' Matt said.

Caro turned round. 'Where? Let me see.'

'It's all right,' Theo said.

'It's not all right,' said Caro. She ran up to the bathroom and got the stuff for burns and some bandages.

'It's not as bad as all that,' said Theo, amused.

As his hand was black she had to bathe it first. It was burnt across the palm, all red and blistery. Caro put the ointment on carefully and then bandaged it up. Alix watched, red-eyed and silent. They all watched.

Bernadette said, 'That was getting my dolly burnt your hand, wasn't it, Theo? I wish you'd left it.'

'Poor old Jemima, get her out of my pocket, Bernadette,' said Theo. 'See if she's got any wig left.'

'She's not Jemima,' Bernadette said. 'She's called Jacqueline.'

Theo laughed. 'Well, how is she?'

'Not bad, considering her accident,' said Caro. 'Heavens! Look at the time! I mustn't be late with Madame's dinner.'

The evening continued to be chaotic and confused. Theo could not manage to bath the boys with his burnt hand, so Alix and Matt did it between them. Caro was a little late with dinner and Madame was irritable; since the children had come she was suspicious as to what was going on in the other part of the house, and if things did not go smoothly she immediately began to blame Theo for upsetting her household. Theo found it so difficult to manipulate his meal with only one burnt hand that he came out to the kitchen afterwards to have some more in peace.

Alix came with him. She sat near him and tried to help, cutting things up, and even pushing them into his spoon for him. She was very contrite and humble.

'Have you forgiven me, Uncle Theo?' she asked him at last.

'Of course I have, Allie dear,' he said, giving her a kiss. 'I'm sorry if I was too cross before. I was frightened of what might have happened.'

'I'm so, so glad Noel is all right,' Alix said.

'Look here, we must all go to bed,' said Caro. 'Or we'll never be up when Dom Richard Houghton comes.'

Dom Richard Houghton was a Benedictine monk who was coming from his monastery to say morning mass for them on Christmas Day. Theo had decided it was too difficult to take the children out, and better for them not to have midnight mass, so this was what had been arranged. They had spent yesterday cleaning and polishing up the chapel ready for the feast, and it now looked, and smelt, quite different from the day when Matt had walked into it by accident and thought no one ever came there. Madame knew what had been done, but she would make no comment.

'It's Christmas Eve!' Matt said. 'It really is!'

'The first Christmas here I've ever enjoyed,' Theo observed.

'Oh Theo,' said Caro, not believing him.

'It is,' he said.

'Even with your hand burnt?' said Alix, still feeling guilty.

'That will soon mend,' said Theo. 'It's been so very well looked after!'

13

The Fate of a Ring

AT eight o'clock in the morning they were all ready for mass, wearing their best clothes, and the winter sun had just risen, and shone in redly through the windows of the chapel. Caro had lighted stoves there, so it was quite warm. There were Christmas roses at the back of the altar, and new beeswax candles in the candlesticks. Dom Richard Houghton said they were to sing the mass, and so they did, and Matt was quite surprised at the tuneful noise they made. Bernadette had a good piping little voice and sang Kyrie just as well, perhaps better than the popular songs she was so fond of. Caro sang and Theo sang and Alix sang and Mickey sang, and Noel made a peculiar humming noise and evidently thought he was singing. Price was there, in his Sunday blue suit, and more words came out of him singing than ever came out of him talking.

But Madame was not there.

Dom Richard had breakfast with them in the kitchen. He was an upright old man with short silvery hair and a kind brown face and Matt thought he looked very much like Saint Benedict himself must have looked. After breakfast he got up and said, 'Well, now I am going to see Louise. Will you go and warn her, Mademoiselle?'

Mademoiselle Tousselin was agitated.

'But it is possible Madame does not want to see you, Dom Richard.'

'But I am going to see her,' said the old monk with calm determination.

Alix followed him into the house and presently she came running back.

'I say! What do you think he said to Gran'mère as he went into her room?'

'What?' asked Matt.

Alix giggled. 'He said, "Louise, you are a very obstinate woman, but if you imagine you can outlast Almighty God, you are just a fool."'

'Good gracious!' said Caro.

'He's known her for years,' said Theo. 'Since before she was married and before he was a monk. That's why I wrote and asked if he could come.'

When Dom Richard came down again everyone was eager to hear what had happened.

He shook his head. 'She is very determined,' he said. 'And yet in a way I have a feeling that she is tired of this long battle against God, against life. She would like to end it, but she cannot see how to end it without giving in, and that is still too much for her pride. It's so difficult to admit we have been wrong! We would rather be unhappy than admit it, and she is not happy. But let's hope she will receive the grace to humble herself in time, at any rate before she comes to die. All of you must pray for her.'

Price drove him away in the old Rolls Royce and the excitement of Christmas Day began.

In spite of the fire there were still presents left for everyone, enough to go round, and plenty of sweets and nuts and tangerines to make up. Caro was very busy, but they all helped her. Madame had told her already that she detested Christmas Day and was staying in her room, so that they were all able to have dinner together, even Mademoiselle joining them, a little nervous and guilty at being in the cheerful company of the kitchen, though obviously enjoying the warmth and the change of conversation. She even pulled crackers with Mickey, an indefatigable cracker-puller, and submitted to wearing a paper hat when Alix crowned her with a vivid red, white and blue tricorne.

In the evening they lit up the tree and the crib and sang carols in the candlelight, and then they played all the games they could think of that could be played sitting down, and at last, very full and sleepy they went off to bed and slept and slept till late the next morning.

This was Boxing Day and the Hartnolls were coming to dinner in the evening. It was mostly a cold meal and after she had got it ready Caro changed into a very pretty frock with a full skirt; it was red, and Caro always looked nice in that bright warm colour.

'Why are you dressing up?' Matt asked her.

'Because Jasper is coming with his family,' she said. 'And he was going to ask his father again about marrying me, so I must look nice in case I have to meet Sir Godfrey.'

She put on her engagement ring and some ear-rings Jasper had given her, but round her throat she wore a pretty gold locket that had belonged to her mother.

'You look lovely,' Matt said.

Theo seemed to think so too. He had been putting Noel and Mickey to bed and met Caro by the back stairs. He gazed at her in admiration so long that Caro went pink in the face and laughed a little.

'Do you like my dress, Theo?' she said, lightly, twirling round at the top of the stairs.

'It's beautiful, and so are you,' he said.

Caro laughed and ran downstairs.

'It's all for Sir Godfrey's benefit,' said Matt gloomily,

and told Theo what Caro had said. 'Don't you hate Jasper, Theo?'

'Yes,' said Theo simply. 'I can't think why she likes him.'

They went downstairs, united by their wonder at Caro's behaviour in wanting to marry Jasper Hartnoll.

Theo was wearing evening dress, of course, in which he always looked uncomfortable and awkward, liable to burst at the seams at any moment, whereas both Sir Godfrey and his son looked at their best in theirs, perfectly at ease. Matt watched them arrive through the glass panels of the baize door. Alix was with him, because her grandmother had said this was not a party for children. Alix did not mind. She said she would help Caro, but she was rather a casual helper. Bernadette was more useful.

'I must say Jasper is terribly handsome,' said Alix, with a sigh. 'How splendid they will look at the wedding, won't they?'

Matt scowled at the prospect and would not answer.

Agnes, who had not come on Christmas day, had arrived after tea to help with dinner as usual.

'Whatever's Mr Ayre done to his hand, his proper hand?' she said.

So then they told her about the fire and she was suitably impressed by the story.

'And that reminds me, Agnes,' said Caro. 'Mind you bring Mr Ayre's plate to the hatch, and lay an extra spoon in case he needs it, will you? We don't want any of Madame's cutting remarks tonight.'

She was in high spirits and wanted everything to go well and everyone to be happy.

Unfortunately they all looked the opposite, Matt thought, squinting through the hatch. Sir Godfrey looked stiffer than usual, Lady Hartnoll was red-eyed, as if she had been crying, Jasper was sulky, and Theo looked the picture of gloom. Only Freda Hartnoll seemed to be enjoying herself, tucking heartily into her food.

After dinner, while the family were having coffee, Caro was expecting Jasper to come and fetch her. She tidied her hair, put on some more lipstick, and waited. But time went by, half an hour went by, and he did not come. Agnes had gone home.

'Matt, you ought to go to bed,' said Caro. Alix had already been sent off.

'Oh no, please, not till I know how it's gone.'

He saw that she was about to argue the point, but just then Jasper came in.

Caro jumped up. 'Oh, Jasper, I thought you were never coming! I'm quite ready.'

Matt thought Jasper looked nervous and sheepish.

'Caroline darling,' he said. 'Would you mind very much if you didn't meet my father tonight?'

'Why? What's happened?' Caro said. 'Jasper, don't say you haven't talked to him about us?'

'No, I have, and that's just it,' he said. 'He's still terribly angry. I didn't dare tell him you were here. He says if I marry you he'll stop my allowance and cut me out of his will.'

'Oh darling,' said Caro with sympathy. 'How very annoying for you! But still, we can easily earn our own living.'

'You don't understand,' said Jasper. 'I would lose my job in the firm too.'

'How unfair!' cried Caro. 'But of course you'll easily get another and do so well your father will want to ask you back! It will be fun proving to him what we can do on our own.'

Jasper cleared his throat. 'Caroline, we must be realistic,' he said. 'It's just stupid to throw away all my chances like that.'

Caro stared at him. 'What do you mean?' she said slowly. 'What do you want to do, then?'

'Well, honestly darling, do you mind if we wait a little longer? I don't want to get across the old man like that.'

'Yes, I do mind,' said Caro. 'You're obviously never going to convince him. The way to do it is to show him you mean what you say. He will respect your judgement then, and your courage.'

'Darling Caroline, you're so impossibly romantic,' said Jasper. 'But it would be madness to throw away everything like that. Without Father behind us we'd just be a couple of poor strugglers.'

'Well, I'm used to that,' said Caro.

'It's not good enough, darling.'

Caro said slowly, 'Jasper, what you mean is, you can live without me but not without your Jaguar.'

Jasper laughed. 'Now don't make a scene out of it, darling, please.'

'No,' said Caro coldly. 'I won't. I think you had better be free to marry someone your father approves.' She took off her engagement ring and put it on the table. 'There you are. I don't want it any more.'

'Caroline!' Jasper cried, but Matt thought he looked just a little relieved, in spite of his outcry.

Caro said, 'Yes, I know I'm right. We should never be happy together, Jasper. We're too different.'

She took off her ear-rings and put them on the table one after the other, beside the ring. 'Take them.'

'Darling, don't be ridiculous,' Jasper said. 'You'll

understand my point of view if you think about it. Please keep the ear-rings.'

'I understand your point of view perfectly,' said Caro. 'I may be silly and sentimental, but I can't help that. Go and find someone who isn't and marry her and enjoy yourself with all your father's money. Good-bye.'

She stalked out of the room and they heard her going up the back stairs.

'Well, I don't know,' said Jasper uncertainly, looking at Matt, who had sat scowling at him throughout the interview. 'Perhaps she's right.' He started to go and then came back and picked up the jewellery. 'May as well take these for the present.'

He slipped them in his pocket and hurried away.

Matt ran upstairs to find Caro. She was sitting very upright on her bed, staring straight in front of her.

'Caro!' said Matt. 'I'm so glad you're not going to marry Jasper!'

'Oh, Matt, come and give me a hug, I feel lonely,' Caro said.

They sat on the bed and hugged each other.

'I had a feeling something was wrong all the time,' said Caro. 'Especially after I came here. Somehow it showed him up, being with his family. I couldn't bear to be married to anyone so spineless and dependent on comfort.'

'I can't think why you ever thought you could,' said Matt.

Caro said, 'He seemed nice at first. Besides, when people keep telling me they love me I begin to feel mean not to love anyone, so I thought perhaps it had better be Jasper, but it never quite worked, although I tried hard to make it. Oh, I am relieved to be free of him, Matt!'

Matt laughed with glee and hugged her again.

'Now we can do anything we like,' he said. 'You could be a cook in Theo's school.'

'They've got a cook,' Caro pointed out. 'And oh, dear Matt, now I shan't be able to send you to the university after all.'

'I don't want to go,' said Matt. 'I'd like to be a doctor and help to cure people.'

'But darling, that's even more expensive.'

'Well, if I can't win grants I'll do something else,' said Matt. 'I don't care, so long as you're not married to someone horrid, like Jasper.'

Caro went downstairs again to wash up the coffee cups, but she told Matt to go to bed. He heard the Hartnoll's car drive away and raised a silent cheer. Then Caro came upstairs again and said good-night and went to her room.

Matt suddenly remembered he had left a glass jar of watersnails in Theo's bathroom. He had been showing them to Noel and Mickey. But now he remembered how snails always seem to get out of jars and crawl all over the place. Caro would be annoyed and perhaps Theo might not like snails in his bathroom. Matt decided to go and see to it before Theo came to bed, so he got up and padded quitely along the passages in his slippers and dressing-gown.

But he found Theo already in his bathroom carefully catching the snails, who were exploring the linoleum floor, and the walls too.

'Oh, my snails!' said Matt, aghast.

'Yours, are they?' said Theo. 'Come and help catch them, then.'

He was wearing only a dressing-gown and Matt was impressed by the amount of hair on his chest.

'You have a look under the bath,' said Theo. 'Easier for you than for me.'

Matt knelt and then lay down on the floor and retrieved a wandering snail. Theo scooped one off the wall.

'Theo,' said Matt, from the floor. 'Caro's decided not to marry Jasper.'

Theo dropped the snail smack on the floor.

'What's that?'

'She's given him back his ring,' said Matt, and told the story.

Theo picked up the snail absently and dropped it back in the jar.

'Is she very unhappy, Matt?'

'No,' said Matt. 'She's wondering why she ever thought of marrying him. So perhaps she could marry you, now.'

Theo smiled. 'I'm afraid it isn't as easy as that,' he said. 'But still, it's good to think she's not tied to him any more. What are you going to do with all these creatures?'

'Put something on top of the jar,' said Matt.

They found a lid for the snails and then Theo told Matt to go back to bed, so he went. He heard Theo whistling in the bathroom, so he knew he was pleased.

14

Cold North Gate

MATT woke rejoicing to the fact of Caro's freedom. It made everything happier and more fun and for the next few days all seemed to go well. They were very busy, with the children to look after, and Alix spent nearly all her time with them, though she began to be nervous because her grandmother was growing suspicious of her frequent absences.

A couple of days after Christmas it began to snow, and one morning at the end of the year Matt woke to find all the world gone white, and the reflected light shining on his ceiling. He suddenly felt a great desire to see the Rose Round in the snow and ran out before breakfast, going through the wood alone. Only birds' feet had printed the pure cover of snow; neat little pronged tracks showed where they had hopped about. The house in the tree had a snow roof and looked suddenly like somebody's home.

Matt had quite a job to open the old door, wedged with drifts of frozen snow, but soon he had squeezed through and was in the garden. No flowers now, only the box borders, loaded with snow, and the yew hedge, looking almost black against the white ground. He went through the gap.

Yes, there it was, the Rose Round, bare, how bare now, not a leaf on the rose trees, not a bud. Nor was the fountain playing. The water in the basin was frozen solid and powdered with snow, like a bowl of meringue and sugar.

Matt stood and looked from afar, hardly liking to tramp over the white lawn. But then he saw a fat bird hopping there and decided he would go after all, to look at the frozen fountain. He walked slowly across the buried grass and the snow creaked under his heels. It was very cold; his breath hung in clouds in the air.

He went up to the fountain and cleared the snow off with his hand, and his hand tingled, touching the cold stuff. The ice underneath was thick and clear like glass. Stuck in it, enclosed, was one white petal, brown at the edges, like a flower inside a glass paper-weight. Matt gazed at it for some time and then up at the gateway that looked to the north, where the white roses grew in summer. Now the archway was rimmed and garlanded with a white fur of snow, edging every wire and every twig with a shining outline. It was beautifully done, just by the falling of the flakes from the sky, and Matt crunched quietly down the invisible path to look at it more closely.

'North,' he murmured. 'To the North Pole.'

North was Scotland, and the far islands, and then nothing but water and icebergs, the northern lights, the midnight sun, the frozen pole, and above the pole the high North Star, by which men had found their way at night for so many hundreds of years.

Cold and hard and strong the north wind blew through the arch, blowing a powder of snow against him, biting his ears and knees, drying his lips.

But as he turned from it the sun came out, low, silver, suddenly dazzling in his eyes, and in the brilliance of that winter light he thought he saw an eagle on the fountain, a white eagle with wings spread for flight and beak uplifted, like the Ayres' eagle on the crumbling stone posts of the gates.

Matt gasped and put his hand up to shade his eyes, but now no eagle was there.

'Hullo Matt,' he heard Theo say behind him and turned again and saw him come through the north arch. A bare rose spray caught his hair and spilled snow over his head like icing sugar.

'I thought I saw an eagle,' Matt said, still dazed. 'A white one.'

'Do you mean this?' said Theo. He came and scraped away the snow at the foot of the fountain and Matt saw that what he had thought was just a carved pattern really included the shape of an eagle, but worn now and indistinct.

'Why, I never noticed that in the summer,' he said. 'Is that your eagle, Theo?'

Theo laughed. 'No, it's St John's,' he said.

'St John's?'

'You know the four Evangelists have signs?' Theo said. 'St John has the eagle, which was said to fly un-blinded towards the sun, because he is the one who looked longest and deepest at Christ on earth and into the mystery of his being when he went back into his glory.'

'What does St Matthew have?' Matt asked.

'He has a Man, a winged Man,' said Theo. 'Christ was the son of Man as well as the Son of God.'

'St Mark has the lion I suppose,' said Matt. 'The Lion of St Mark. But why does he?'

'Jesus was called the Lion of Judah too,' said Theo. 'The lion is the king of beasts, the most splendid of the wild beasts, and Christ was the true king of Israel, and of the whole race of men, but people did not recognize him, because he came in the disguise of a poor man and gave himself up to die the death of a slave. People still don't recognize him, but he is the King all the same.'

Matt remembered how he had seen the lion when he had dreamed (was it a dream?) of the south gate and its way through to the deserts and jungles of the world, the red rose gate. Perhaps it was the way through to the dangers and passions that trouble everyone alive on earth, and brought even the King to death, though he was innocent. And hadn't there been his own face, but wise and ancient, a winged face looking to the west, across the seas of tears and yearning?

'Are they all here, all the signs?' he asked.

'Yes, on the base of the fountain,' said Theo.

'Who put them there?'

'My father,' said Theo. 'When he found the statue of Our Lady for the fountain.'

'And what's St Luke, Theo?'

'St Luke is a Bull.'

'How queer! Why?' Matt asked.

'I'm not sure,' said Theo. 'Perhaps because the Bull is a sign of life: the zodiac bull comes in the spring, you know. He's the sign of generation and Christ is the regenerator of man, and his sacrifice of his own life was made in the spring. He said himself that the seed must die to bring up the new corn. It's all a mystery, you know. The signs are symbols of the mystery: they let you look through the doors but they don't tell you everything at once. You can never know everything there is to know, that's why we shall be happy for ever in heaven if we get there.'

The sun shone round them on the snow, so dazzling that Matt blinked.

'The eagle's in the north,' he said.

He looked at Theo's hand on the edge of the basin. He had left off Caro's bandage and only had plaster over the burnt place of his palm. But what Matt noticed now was the sun glinting on gold, on a ring he wore on his little finger.

'Why are you wearing a ring, Theo?' he asked.

'I always used to wear it,' said Theo. 'But last year I lost it, I'm always losing things. I found it yesterday in an old shoe in my cupboard, so I thought I'd put it on again.'

Matt peered at it. 'It's a signet, isn't it?' The ring had a red stone, dull and opaque.

'Yes,' said Theo. 'That's got our eagle on it. Take it off and look, if you like.'

Matt pulled the ring off Theo's finger and examined it. He saw the tiny eagle engraved on the red stone.

'Why is it an eagle?' he said, putting the ring back on Theo's hand.

'I suppose some Ayre thought it would be a splendid thing to have the king of the birds for a crest, the king of the air,' said Theo, smiling. 'With a name like that, you see.'

'Not because of St John?'

'I'm afraid probably not,' said Theo. 'But we can think of it as St John's if we like, can't we? What are you doing out so early?'

'I just wanted to see the Rose Round in the snow.'

'Just what I felt,' said Theo. 'But you mustn't miss your breakfast and I certainly don't want to miss mine.'

'Caro would keep it for us,' Matt said.

'But we don't want to put her routine out and make her work too hard,' said Theo.

He went with Matt into the wood, heaving the old gate open and shut on its complaining hinges.

'Ought to repair that gate, I suppose,' he remarked, as they went away through the wood.

As they came into the kitchen Bernadette said, 'There's a letter for you, Theo, from Sam.'

He took it and opened it and began to read it straight away. Since the children had come Theo always had his breakfast in the kitchen; Madame had hers in bed and Mademoiselle and Alix, by her orders, had to have theirs in the dining-room. Mademoiselle was always nervously admonishing Alix for talking through the hatch. Today everyone was chattering about the snow and Alix was planning toboggan rides at the top of her voice, and Noel was squeaking out, 'I want to see the snowman!' as if snowmen grew out of the ground as soon as it snowed. But Theo stood in the middle of it all not hearing anything, frowning, with the letter in his hand.

'What's happened, Theo?' asked Caro, who was watching him.

He looked up and said, 'The last chance of a house before next term has fallen through. Sam's at his wits' end. He can leave some of the children at their homes temporarily, but not the Number Ones. That's six more besides these three. He doesn't know what to do.'

'Oh dear,' said Caro. 'Will they have to go to some other home, then?'

Bernadette and Mickey and Noel all stopped talking at that, and their anxious eyes turned towards Theo. Matt thought how awful it would be to have no one belonging to you, so that you never knew when you might not be packed off to strangers.

Theo looked at them too. 'No,' he said slowly. 'We shall have to bring the others here.'

'Hooray!' cried Mickey. 'Three cheers for Woodhall St Raphael!'

'But Theo, what will Madame say?' Matt asked. 'She doesn't like having even three children, let alone nine.'

'All the same, they must come,' said Theo. 'It would be

wicked not to take them in when we so easily can. We'll
have them all in the end. We'll start the school again in the
summer, but just for this term it will be the nine Number
Ones, so that Mamma can have time to get used to it.'

'Will you really be able to do that, Uncle Theo?' said
Alix, leaning through the hatch and calling across the
passage.

'Alix! You must not do zis,' said Mademoiselle Tousselin, in great agitation.

'Yes,' said Theo. 'Mamma's rooms are all on the
ground floor, even her bedroom now. We need not use
any of the downstairs of the house, so that she need never
see the children unless she wants to, though I hope she
will want to in the end.' He turned to Caro. 'We'll make a
second kitchen in the big scullery for Mrs Bush and
Betty,' he said. 'We have our own equipment of course.
They will cook for the school and Maggie will do our
housekeeping separate from Mamma's and yours. I hope
you won't mind this invasion too much.'

'Mind! I shall enjoy it,' said Caro. 'Alix, if you've
finished in the dining-room, may we have the plates?
Theo, you haven't eaten anything yet. Here's your bacon
and egg all getting hard in the oven.'

Theo hastily sat down and began to eat. When he was
in the kitchen he used his other hand to help himself,
though with the glove on it. As Bernadette said, her artificial hand was really much more use. But he could just
get hold of a fork with it, to keep things down while he
cut them, though he usually dropped anything if he tried
to lift it. Matt found it hard not to watch him, and watching, wanted to help, but he thought he had better not. It
seemed to be a St Raphael's habit for everyone to do as
much as possible for himself without making a fuss. Even

Noel, propped up on cushions, made wavering dabs at his mouth with a spoon. His weakly little arms seemed to have very little strength in them and his control of his hands was vague and spasmodic, but he liked trying to do what everyone else did.

From then on everyone was more busy than ever. Theo sent a telegram to Sam after breakfast and then he and Matt and Alix began lighting fires in empty rooms upstairs and collecting blankets and sheets to air. Theo dragged mattresses from beds long unused and propped them up against chairs in front of the fires. When they had been working away for some time Theo said they must not miss the snow and told them to go off and play.

'You come too,' Matt said.

Theo said he would come in the afternoon. So Matt and Alix went off to make a toboggan, and this took them the rest of the time till lunch. They used two old skis for the base, which Alix said had belonged to her father, Theo's brother Julian. The toboggan would hardly have been ride-worthy had not Price lent a hand. Alix told him about the children coming.

'Mr Ayre has the right idea,' Price said. 'And this house is big enough to take a school as well as his own family, if he should marry and have one.'

Alix laughed. 'Who would marry Uncle Theo?' she said.

'Whoever did would get a good husband,' said Price.

Alix giggled. 'But a very funny-looking one!' she said.

'Looks isn't everything in life, Miss Alix,' said Price sternly.

Alix made a face, but she did not argue with Price.

At lunch-time Theo broke the news to his mother. Matt heard because he was fetching the plates as usual from the hatch. Theo explained in his slow way what had happened, who was coming and why, while the old lady interrupted with cries of dismay and horror, in English and French.

'But you cannot do this to me, Théodore!' she exclaimed finally.

'I promise we shan't be a nuisance to you, Mamma,' said Theo.

Madame fixed her beady eyes on him.

'Very well,' she said. 'I shall hold you responsible for whatever is done.'

'All right,' said Theo, not apparently alarmed to shoulder all the possible sins and mistakes of St Raphael's School.

Matt skipped back to the kitchen and told Caro.

'Good for Theo,' she said. 'He surprises me, sometimes. When he makes up his mind, no one can budge him. Perhaps that's what Madame finds so irritating; he's as obstinate as she is in his own way! And yet I believe he's still afraid of her.'

'No wonder,' said Matt, thinking of the interview he had overheard in the summer, knowing how unkind Madame could be if she wanted to.

Caro came out with them in the afternoon; they all went, Theo carrying Noel, who was rolled up in a rug and had a red cap on his head so that he looked more like a gnome than ever. Matt and Alix dragged their home-made toboggan, 'one dog to each rope,' as Caro said. They dragged it up beyond Bertrand's Tower and then slid down the steep slope the other side of the ridge. They gave Bernadette rides too, and she got very excited, screaming out, 'Oo! It's as good as the scenic!' every time they went over a bump. They even got Mickey out of his chair and with Caro's help gave him a ride down the lower part of the slope.

Those who were not riding helped to build a snowman for Noel. Theo fetched an old wicker settee out of Bertrand's Tower, pointing out to Caro that if she had had her way this would have been thrown away instead of coming in so useful now. She only laughed. Theo wedged Noel on to it, so that he himself could help with the snowman and the tobogganing. He was a useful dog, as Alix observed, a giant dog, but he would not have a ride for fear of breaking the toboggan. This turned out to be a wise precaution, for at last one of the struts gave as Matt and Alix were whizzing over a bump and the toboggan stood abruptly on its nose, flinging the children headfirst into flurries of snow. No one was really hurt, only breathless and bruised, but after that they had to stick to snowman building. They made a snow wife and three snow children for the snowman, much to Noel's delight.

Matt helped Theo to carry the wicker settee back to Bertrand's Tower, and they pushed it into a corner with all the other junk. There was the alabaster Virgin still standing among the rubbish, poised on the points of the moon, smiling in the cold air of winter.

'We must find a better place for her,' Theo said.

They went out again and Theo took Noel from Caro, 'The Noel chrysalis' as Alix called him, because he was so rolled up in his rug, and they all went down the slope towards the house. At the garden door that opened on the terrace a small black figure was standing.

'Madame is watching,' said Caro.

'Poor Mamma,' said Theo. 'If only she would give up this miserable pose, how she would enjoy the children! I believe it's now little more than a habit, but it's such a very long-standing habit.'

'Like her habit of saying unkind things to you,' said Caro.

'She probably doesn't mean all she says,' Theo said.

The small black figure went into the house and the door was shut.

They all went round to the kitchen and had an enormous tea of toast and dripping and slabs of farmhouse cake, but Alix had to go and change her frock and have tea with her grandmother. Afterwards they heard the music of the harp, as Alix practised for her lesson with Mr Howell.

'Isn't she clever?' said Bernadette, with admiration. 'And beautiful as – as a mermaid!'

They all laughed at the comparison, but Theo said, 'She's getting less of a mermaid, thank goodness.'

'What do you mean, Theo?' asked Matt.

'Less cold-blooded, he means,' said Caro. 'More warm-hearted, don't you?'

Theo nodded and went off to turn the airing mattresses round, and Matt went to help him.

'When are they coming, Theo?' he asked.

'In a few days, I hope.'

And in a few days come they did, Sam and Maggie and Mrs Bush and her daughter Betty and all six of the Number Ones, as Sam called the orphans who had no homes of their own. At first Matt found it peculiar seeing so many cripples all at once; he began to feel as if everyone in the world had something wrong, or as if he were a freak with his two arms and two legs, running about free and careless. But as soon as he got to know each child, by name and by nature, he began to get used to the situation and presently hardly noticed it. He had come to think of them as people and not as cripples.

In a way now he was less with the children, because Sam and Maggie organized them all in the rooms Theo had arranged for them. Maggie was a plump smiling person with soft brown hair, and she evidently regarded the nine orphans as her own special family; some of the smaller ones called her Mum quite often and she liked that. The others called her Maggie, just as they called Theo by his Christian name. They seemed to have a lot of fun upstairs, judging by the laughter. Mrs Bush and Betty cooked for them in the scullery and they had their meals upstairs, because it was easier to carry the food up than to carry the children down.

Sam Kingston was still writing to estate agents about houses, but Theo said, 'You're here to stay.'

15

Alix Kept Down

ALIX was not able to enjoy the beginning of St Raphael's at Woodhall. Her grandmother had seen her out with Theo and Caro and the children on that snowy day and she forbade her then to go into the other part of the house, or to play with Matt, or to speak to the Kingstons and their charges. Alix pleaded and stormed in vain: the old lady was adamant. Yet Alix might have refused to obey had not Mrs Ayre found an effective threat.

Alix wrote to Matt: 'I have had to promise not to see you because if I don't Grandemère will send me to stay with Aunt Phyllis, the Hartnolls, you know. I am furious and it's not fair and Uncle Theo is no use at all. He asked me not to make a fuss because of the children. I believe he cares more about them than he does about me, his own niece, and you can tell him so from me. Nobody cares what I feel and Grandemère is a tyrant. I'll find out some way to defy her, see if I don't. Tyrants ought to be defied.'

She pushed this note under the baize door. Theo was with Matt when he found it, and Matt showed him what Alix had written about him.

'Poor Alix,' said Theo, frowning in a worried way. 'It's too bad to shut her away now. She may not have realized before how lonely she was, but after all the fun she has had lately it must seem very hard to her.'

'She sounds very angry about it,' said Matt, dubiously.

'She's the sort to fight rather than weep,' said Theo, smiling. 'I hope she doesn't break out too disastrously.'

Matt saw Alix sometimes, stalking angrily alone on the terrace, or going off for a ride with Price. It was annoying, but much worse for her than for him. He had plenty to do, and the days before school began again were going all too quickly.

One day Madame went out to tea at the Hartnolls' house, and Alix begged Theo so hard to let her have tea with Matt that he gave in, and came with her. Alix was quite shy at first, perhaps because she had been so much alone with the two old ladies, but she soon thawed and was chattering away merrily when Theo said it was time for her to go back to Mademoiselle.

'Oh, it's so unfair!' she cried. 'Why should I?'

'I know it's unfair,' said Theo. 'But if you are obedient and good, perhaps Mamma will change her mind.'

'You know she won't,' Alix said. 'She's always unfair to you, and nothing makes her change her mind, however much you try to please her.'

'I'm afraid that's true,' Caro remarked.

'Even if it is true, I don't see what we can do about it,' said Theo.

'Agnes says, "What the eye don't see the heart don't grieve over,"' said Alix. 'I shall just come whenever I can.'

'I don't think you ought to do that when you promised not to,' said Theo.

'Oh, don't be so pi, Uncle Theo!' she cried. 'What am I doing now if I'm not breaking my promise?'

'I'm breaking it for you, this time,' he said, smiling. 'But just for once, because Matt is going soon.'

'Yes, and what's the use of just one tea in the kitchen?' Alix grumbled.

'Well, give me a chance!' said Theo. 'I'm hoping to

persuade Mamma that Matt is good for you, since he has much better manners and is altogether more reasonable than you are.'

Alix made a face at Matt and laughed.

'Come on, now, Alix,' Theo said. 'If Mamma finds you have come here with me she will be angry with both of us, and that won't help.'

'Why are you so frightened of her?' said Alix cheekily. 'I'm not frightened. I shall do what I like.'

'Alix, please,' said Theo.

But she was in a perverse mood and thought she had plenty of time to waste delaying and teasing him. Madame, however, had a habit of returning promptly from her rare visits. She arrived home and found Mademoiselle Tousselin alone. Poor timid Mademoiselle admitted that 'Monsieur Théodore' had fetched Alix to have tea with him in the kitchen.

Madame at once came stalking through the baize door, and before they had realized she had come home there she was in the kitchen, small and upright, and very angry.

'Alix! So, you break your promise,' she said. 'You will go and stay at the Hartnolls' till this boy has left the house.'

'Oh please, Gran'mère, don't send me there!' Alix cried.

'Mamma, it's my fault,' said Theo anxiously.

'As if I could not guess that!' said Madame. 'Always from a child you find your friends among the servants. But you shall not teach Alix such habits.'

Alix turned scarlet. 'Gran'mère! Don't say things like that! Caro and Matt are just as good as we are, better than we are.'

'Egalitarian nonsense!' said Madame, not at all abashed. 'Miss Rendal knows I have respect for her, but I am sure she also knows that it is not suitable for you to play with her brother.'

Caro said, 'I don't see why they shouldn't, Madame. My father certainly never owned a big house like this, his family were farmers and he was a schoolmaster, but I think he was your equal in learning and culture, and if that doesn't give us a common background, what does?'

'So that is what you think, is it, Mademoiselle?' said the old lady, looking at Caro with her piercing beady eyes. 'Well, let me tell you that I do not think it. Come, child.' She tapped her cane on the floor.

'But Gran'mère, need I go to the Hartnolls'?' Alix pleaded. 'You said it was Uncle Theo's fault more than mine.'

Matt thought this was unfair of Alix; she knew she could always deflect her grandmother's anger to Theo. So her boasted bravery only came to this, he thought, letting Theo take the consequences of her own silliness.

'That is true,' said Madame. 'Why should you be punished for what he has persuaded you to do? Theo, of course, is too old to be punished. We cannot forbid him to amuse himself in the kitchen, but perhaps we can warn Miss Rendal that if we hear too much of this visiting, she will have to leave us.'

Both Theo and Caro flushed red at this, and had nothing to say. The old lady stalked out in triumph, Alix followed her demurely, but with a rebellious look in her eye.

'I'm sorry, Caro,' Theo said at last, after an uncomfortable pause. 'My mother has a genius for insult. Please forget it if you can.'

'It doesn't matter in the least,' said Caro, in a sharp, flippant tone that astonished Matt. She began quickly and noisily clearing up the tea-things. 'Naturally, with her ideas of class she imagines I'd be a fool not to make the most of my chances.' She laughed, smacking the plates together, not looking at Theo. 'You needn't worry, Mr Ayre, I haven't the slightest intention of entangling you with cunning wiles. I never asked you to come in here, and you can tell her that next time she makes such a ridiculous suggestion.'

Theo looked miserable, mumbled something about Noel's bedtime, and went hurriedly away.

'Suggesting I was angling for a proposal!' said Caro crossly. 'The aristocratic old demon!' She slammed the bread in its bin.

'But why did you say that to Theo? He hated it,' said Matt. 'He really does want to marry you.'

'What nonsense!' said Caro.

'But he does,' Matt said. 'He told me ages ago, by mistake. He said he knew it was silly for someone like him to fall in love with you, but he couldn't help it.'

Caro turned red in the face and began putting things away in a great hurry.

'Well, if he ever did feel like that it was a stupid idea,' she said. 'He'd better forget it at once, and so had you.'

'But why, Caro?' said Matt, disappointed. 'Don't you like him?'

'Oh yes, Theo's all right,' Caro said. 'He's just not the sort of person I've ever thought of marrying.'

'Why not? What sort of person ought he to be?'

'Oh, Matt, you can't possibly understand,' said Caro. 'Do stop going on about it.'

Matt thought she was being very irritating. He fetched his book and gave up talking in favour of reading.

Matt sometimes slipped through the door on the

terrace and into the Library, for he knew Madame hardly ever went there. Theo had long since given him permission to borrow anything he wanted, and as well as the rows of leather-bound volumes there were some shelves at the back with ordinary books on them, rather old ones. The day after Alix's unlucky visit he went there and prowled hopefully round the shelves, nosing into one book after another. He was standing in one of the bays at the end of the Library, with a Jules Verne book in his hands, when he heard the doors click open and Madame's voice saying impatiently, 'Well, Théodore, what is it now?'

Matt, horrified, dived under the table as quietly as he could. But Madame and Theo stayed talking by the door. Matt heard every word, he could not help it.

'Mamma, it's about Alix,' said Theo. 'I know you want to do the best for her. What she needs very much is the companionship of other children.'

'You want me to let her make a friend of that boy,' said Madame. 'But I do not wish her to become a rough hoyden like these modern young misses.'

'Why should playing with Matt turn her into a hoyden?' said Theo, smiling. 'She's much wilder than he is. Why not let her get rid of some of her wildness before she grows up? She has too much spirit to sit by and watch others having all the adventures. She might have the wrong sort of adventures if she knows nothing about people or real life.'

'Nonsense,' said Madame. 'Alix will be beautiful. The world will be at her feet.'

'Will that make her happy?' said Theo.

'Why should she not be happy?' said Madame. 'People will always gather round Alix, as they did with my Julian.'

'Julian wasn't happy either,' said Theo.

Matt, horrified, dived under the table.

'Ah!' cried Madame, annoyed. 'You were always jealous of Julian! He was everything that you were not, my poor Théo. He was born to be a leader of men. What he would not have done!' She sighed.

'All those admiring friends didn't make him happy all the same,' said Theo doggedly. 'And Alix is a girl, so she will be even more unhappy unless she learns how to give as well as take. Let her have a friend like Matt, anyway, it can't do any harm. Do, Mamma, do let her see him while he is here.'

'To please you? Certainly not!' said his mother. 'I suppose you have taken up the boy to flatter that pretty sister of his.'

There was a moment of uncomfortable silence and then Matt, to his relief, heard Theo say firmly, 'I like Matt for his own sake.'

'Oh, very likely!' said Madame sarcastically. 'She is certainly a pretty girl, Théo, and she seems to be succeeding in turning your head.'

Theo said, 'I wish you hadn't said that to Caro, Mamma. It wasn't fair to her, or to me.'

'It would not be fair to let a shrewd girl make a fool of you, Théo,' said his mother. 'But perhaps I am wrong. No doubt such a pretty young woman knows she could make a better bargain. After all, she must know you have no fortune behind this house of ours, and without money why should she marry a man like you, and with that unfortunate deformity too?'

Matt heard Theo walk across the room to the window. He had a feeling that, as usual, Theo was more hurt by Madame's words than she realized. But when he spoke he ignored what she had said and patiently went back to the problem he wanted to discuss.

'About Alix, Mamma. I wonder if you realize how dangerous it is to thwart her like this? She knows it is an unfair rule and if you force her to obey she may do something silly to show her independence.

'So you think she will defy me?' said Madame. 'No doubt, since you encourage and teach her to break her promises. I am shocked at that, Théo. But as for Miss Alix, I think I have the stronger will.'

'Don't make it a battle of wills, Mamma, please,' Theo said.

Madame gave a little snort of laughter.

'You say that because you've never had a will of your own, Théo,' she said. 'The child has more spirit than you ever had.'

'Leave me out of it,' said Theo, exasperated. 'It's nothing to do with me.'

'It certainly is nothing to do with you,' said his mother. 'Julian's child is in my charge and I will do as I think best for her. As for Alix herself, I don't think she is very grateful for your interest. She laughs at you, Théo.'

'I know what she feels like, all the same,' said Theo sadly. 'I know what it's like to be a lonely child in this house.'

Matt heard Madame tapping her cane on the floor.

'I am bored with this complaining of yours, Théodore,' she said. 'I do not understand such grumbling and interference. Enough, now. It is cold in here. Open the door for me, if you please.'

Theo went to open the door. He did not go out with her but came back and paced slowly down the middle of the room. In the bay opposite Matt was the fireplace, empty of course, where the picture of Bertrand Ayre hung on the wall. Theo went and leant his elbows on the high marble mantelpiece and put his head down on his arms with a long, angry sigh.

Matt did not quite know what to do, but he did not want to hide from Theo, so after a moment he came out from under the table and began apologizing.

Theo turned round, startled, and then laughed.

'You would make a good spy, Matt!' he said. 'I never knew you were there.'

'I didn't mean to spy, Theo, honestly,' said Matt anxiously. 'I am sorry you didn't persuade Madame about Alix, though.'

'So am I,' said Theo. 'I hope Alix won't do anything silly, either.' He looked at Matt's book. '"The Secret of the Island." Isn't that the one where the whole island blows up at the end, but everyone who matters is all right?'

They went out of the Library together, but Theo did not come through to the kitchen. He went straight upstairs to the St Raphael's rooms. He had not been near Caro since yesterday's incident, nor did he come that day, nor the next, and if Matt wanted to see him he had to look for him upstairs. He did not dare to ask Theo why he did not come, because he knew it was Caro's cross words that kept him away.

On the third day after Madame's visit to the kitchen Matt went upstairs to his own room after tea, because he was tired of Agnes's chatter, all about people he did not know. It was cold in his little room, so he lit the paraffin stove Theo had put there for him and got out his drawing and painting things and settled down to make a picture. It was to be a picture of a man fishing in a river, and he got very absorbed in it. It was dark outside now, but he had not bothered to draw the curtains. The sash window was open at the top to let out the paraffin fumes.

Suddenly he heard a whistle in the dark outside. He cocked his head. A whistle again, rather a breathy one.

Matt went and pushed up the lower window and peered out. The electric bulb above the back door was on, and it lit the bricked yard with a wan cold light. Underneath Matt's window the roof of a narrow building jutted out at right angles to the wall of the house. This was the old wash-house, with the bathroom that Caro and Matt used on top of it. Matt sometimes thought it was rather like the prow of a ship in the dark, with the old chimney as a stumpy funnel.

He could see nothing outside. The yard was empty. The moon was rising in long pearled clouds above the bare black trees beyond.

Suddenly he heard a laugh, away to his right.

'Matt! Here I am!'

He leant out and peered round to his right. He saw Alix, in her blue velvet dress and black dancing-pumps, coming crabwise along a ledge of stone that ran round the back of the house above the windows of the first floor. So he was looking down at her, but not much.

He gasped. 'Alix! What are you doing?' There was an awful sick feeling in his stomach.

'Coming to see you, idiot,' she said. 'I never thought of this before. It's easy, once you get on this ledge.'

Indeed it was easy if you kept your head. The ledge was wide enough and solid, but the drop to the yard was terrifying.

'Oh, do go back!' Matt said, watching her with horrified fascination.

'Don't be silly,' said Alix. 'This ledge runs right to the wash-house roof. I'll just have to climb up that and then I can get in at your window. I'm not going back now.'

In a minute or two she reached the angle between the roof and the wall and stepped across on to the tiles above the gutter, dropping forward on the steeply pitched roof like a cat. Then she came crawling up, looking up at Matt, grinning with triumph.

But she had reckoned without the age and disrepair of the buildings at Woodhall. Suddenly under her feet a broken tile slipped, slid away, dislodging another. Alix lost her grip altogether and with a fearful cry slid down the steep roof to the guttering. A piece of it broke away and fell down with a shattering smash into the yard below, but Alix fetched up sideways with her feet against some that held – for the moment.

There she crouched shuddering, all her nerve gone, and shrieking 'Oh! Oh! Oh!' in a way that made Matt feel he was going to be sick with fright.

16

Danger in the Dark Night

ALIX'S cries of terror brought Caro and Agnes running out of the kitchen into the yard, and Theo from the stables where he had been feeding the horses, because it was Price's day off. They all looked up and saw Alix cowering on the roof in the rotten gutter. Theo ran straight into the house.

Matt had just put his leg over the sill to climb out when Theo came bursting into his room.

'Come back, Matt,' he said. 'Let me do that.'

Much to Matt's surprise he began hastily taking off his shoes and socks.

'Won't slip,' he explained. 'Matt, call Sam and tell him to get out the long ladder from the stables, quick as you can.'

Matt started for the door.

'And Matt!'

'Yes?'

'Ask Maggie for the new clothes line I bought her. It might help.'

He climbed out of the window and Matt ran into the passage. On the stairs he saw Sam Kingston already running down.

'Sam!' he shouted, and gave his message, breathless with panic and hurry.

'Right!' said Sam and disappeared.

Matt ran to the upstairs pantry where, as he had guessed, Maggie was washing up, with two of the girls helping her.

'Oh, quick,' he gasped. 'Alix is stuck on the roof and Theo wants the rope, quick. The clothes line.'

Maggie pulled open a drawer. The clothes line was there, still done up and unused. Matt seized it and started off again.

'Where's Sam?' Maggie cried.

'Gone to get the long ladder,' Matt said as he went. 'From the stables.'

Maggie ran down to help Sam and Matt ran up, back to his room. The curtains were blowing back with the breeze from the open window. Matt, panting, leant out.

Theo was lying spreadeagled on the steep roof, lowering himself slowly down towards Alix and talking to her as he did so. It was easier to see him than Alix, for the moon showed up his white shirtsleeves whereas she was a shadowy heap. She had stopped screaming, but she was shivering and cowering against the tiles.

'Try to reach out your hand to me, Alix,' Theo was saying. He had gone down to the right of her, further away from the wall, so that his left arm, the strong one, was towards her.

'I can't, I can't,' Alix said, too terrified to move.

'All right, stay still, I'm coming,' said Theo. He shifted himself closer to her.

Matt saw that he did not dare to trust his weight to the rotten gutter and it was difficult to reach Alix without getting his feet down on it. He had to lie sideways, with nothing to hold on to, on the old loose tiles. But he managed to take a grip of Alix's nearest arm, above the elbow.

'Now, come on,' he said persuasively. 'Try to get flat on your stomach, like me.'

'No, no,' moaned Alix. 'It'll give way if I move.'

Theo moved closer to her again and changed his grip, putting his arm right across her and grasping her other arm. In this way he was able to get her to move a little, flattening out so that more of her weight was on the roof and less on the gutter. She only had the confidence to do it because he was holding her, but Matt could see that if one false move were made they would both go over together. There was nothing for Theo to hold, and anyway the only hand he could hold with was holding Alix. But for the moment they lay there, not slipping.

Matt saw Sam and Maggie and Caro getting the long ladder out into the yard and slowly beginning to raise it. Sam walked up under it till the narrow end was against the wall, and then they were able to push it.

'Now,' said Theo to Alix. 'We've only got to worm up this bit of roof and then we'll get in at Matt's window.'

'No, no, I can't get up there,' she said. 'I can't, I can't.'

She had completely lost her nerve.

Theo screwed his head round.

'Sam! Have you got the ladder up?'

'Yes,' shouted Sam. 'But it won't reach.'

He was climbing the ladder, hand over hand. Maggie and Caro were holding the foot of it. Agnes was standing gaping upwards with her mouth open. Several of the St Raphael's children, the walking ones, had come into the yard, and they were all staring up too, their pale faces lit by the electric light over the back door. The other side of the yard was a door to the old billiards room and Matt saw a light go on there, and two small black figures hurrying; Madame and Mademoiselle.

'How big's the gap?' Theo called to Sam.

Sam was nearly at the top of the ladder. He held on with one hand and reached up with the other.

'I just can't reach the gutter,' he said. 'About a foot off it.'

Theo looked up again towards Matt.

'Got the line, Matt?'

Matt held up the neat bundle.

'Undo it,' said Theo. 'Tie the end round the bed, give it some half-hitches. Can you do those?'

'Yes,' said Matt. Hastily he undid the line and followed Theo's instructions.

'Now throw me the rest,' said Theo, when he came back to the window.

Matt carefully tossed down the stiff coiled line, with such good aim that it hit Theo in the face.

'Oh, sorry!' he cried, aghast.

'All right,' Theo said. 'Good shot. Now, Alix, you can get over the edge to Sam on the ladder. He's just below, he'll catch your legs and put your feet on it. I'll tie this rope round you, so that even if you slip, you won't fall.'

Matt thought he would much rather have climbed up the roof himself, but Alix evidently found it impossible to do the thing which had proved so terrifying and unsafe before.

Theo flung a loop of the line round the wash-house chimney, and then he began to fix it round Alix, under her arms. It was a difficult, awkward job, even though he propped himself on his elbow and used his deformed hand to help himself. Matt saw he had pulled off the glove he usually wore. It was on the floor beside his shoes and socks.

Eventually it was done, and with guiding shouts from Sam, Alix at length wriggled her feet over the edge. Theo, who was sitting up now with his back to the chimney, held the rope in his good hand, and kept it just taut, so that she should feel safer. It was a nasty moment for Alix when her legs hung over the roof, but Sam caught them at once and guided her feet to the top rung.

'I've got you,' Matt heard him say.

Matt could see Sam helping Alix down, but Theo, paying out the line, could not. Presently it went taut and Sam called out, 'I'm cutting the rope, Theo. Can't manage your knots.'

'Are you down?'

'Not quite. Line's too short.'

Sam cut the line with his penknife and Theo drew it up.

Sam and Alix reached the bottom of the ladder. Caro caught Alix and hugged her tight.

Sam called up. 'Are you coming down, Theo?'

'No fear,' he answered. 'I'm going up. This line would never hold me.'

He was coiling up the line as he spoke and twisted round to get the loop off the chimney. It stuck and he could not get at it.

'Bother the thing,' he said, and turned over so that he was kneeling on the roof, holding on to the chimney with his deformed arm and feeling round it to loosen the rope with his hand.

Suddenly the crumbling brickwork of the whole top of the chimney came away bodily in his arms. Theo fell sideways on the roof and the piece of masonry crashed on the tiles, bouncing down to the edge.

'Look out below!' Theo shouted.

He was slipping as he called out, rapidly slithering down the tiles, grabbing at the rope and missing it.

The top of the chimney fell over the edge of the roof and smashed on the ground far below.

'Oh! Theo! Oh!' cried Matt, horrified, unable to do anything to stop Theo rolling down the roof.

In a few seconds he hit the gutter. The rotten iron crumbled and bent and broke under the impact. Theo clutched at it as he slid over, breaking his fall only for a moment, for it came away in his hand.

He fell right over the roof and on to the ladder. No one was holding the bottom of it now. It rocked as he hit it and fell sideways, the top crashing against the wall of the house, with Theo half on and half off it. After an instant's pause the foot of the ladder slipped in the yard and it came down, and Theo with it.

Matt heard the smack of the wood hitting the ground, and the sickening thump of Theo's body on the bricked yard.

'Theo!' screamed out Caro, rushing towards him.

Matt, petrified, stared down from high above. He saw Theo splayed out on his back across the ladder, Caro's hair shining in the light from the back door as she bent over him, and everyone closing round to see. And on the other side of the yard, in the doorway of the old billiards room, stood Madame, with Mademoiselle behind her, small black figures with white faces.

In that moment of horror Matt saw it all as clear as a picture and then he turned and ran from the room, jumping over Theo's abandoned shoes, and raced downstairs, through the kitchen and out into the yard.

Caro was sitting on her heels, lifting up Theo's head, and Sam was kneeling on the other side of him. Theo lay quite limp and inert and Matt thought he was dead. There was a dreadful hollow inside him.

'He's coming round,' Sam said.

Theo began to make a noise which screwed Matt up

inside with sympathetic pain, groaning, 'Oh, oh, oh,' over and over.

Presently he moved a little and opened his eyes and saw Caro leaning over him, and Sam, and after a moment he stopped groaning, shutting his mouth tight. The light from the door shone on his face, showing up the drops of sweat on his forehead like beads.

'Oh, Sam,' Caro said. 'What can we do? Is he terribly hurt?'

'I think we'd better try to carry him indoors,' said Sam. 'Mags, darling, go and ring up the hospital. Matt, you help Caro with his feet.'

Matt ran to pick up Theo's feet, bare and dirty from the roof, and one was bleeding, cut by the guttering perhaps. But when they tried to move him Theo gasped so painfully that Sam let him down again. Theo shut his eyes and lay still, breathing heavily.

Alix, white-faced, stood beside him.

'Is he going to die?' she said in anguish.

Theo opened his eyes again and looked at her.

'No,' he said hoarsely.

He was the only person who seemed sure enough to say so. Some of the children were crying and Sam's usually cheerful face was drawn tight with anxiety.

Maggie came out from the house, tears running down her cheeks.

'They're sending an ambulance at once,' she said. 'Shan't we move him in out of the cold, Sam?'

'I'm afraid to,' Sam said. 'It seemed to hurt him so much.'

'It's beginning to rain,' said Maggie.

Cold drops fell here and there, and soon after, sleeting drops, neither rain nor snow.

'We must put him on something flat, then,' said Sam. 'Didn't I see an old door when I was fetching the ladder?'

He went to look and called Matt to help him. There was an old frame-and-batten door, with broken hinges, lying there waiting to be repaired. Sam and Matt brought it out into the yard and laid it down beside Theo. The sleet was coming down faster now, and Maggie was shepherding the children inside.

'Now then,' said Sam.

He put his hands under Theo's shoulders, with Caro helping, and Maggie and Matt took hold of his legs under the knees and together they shifted him from the ground to the door. When Matt stood up again there was blood on his hand.

'Oh, look," he said, feeling sick inside.

'I expect his leg's broken,' said Sam. 'I only hope there's nothing worse. Come on, let's get him indoors now.'

It was quite a job; Theo was so heavy. He was too long for the door, his feet hung over the end. But at last they got him into the kitchen and laid him down, door and all, on the old settee where he usually put Noel. Again Theo was too long for it and Matt fetched a chair and put his feet on it.

Now that he was in the light, lying there where they could see him, Matt thought he looked even worse. His shirt was very dirty from the roof and torn, but there was blood on that too and Sam said he must have broken some ribs, if nothing more.

'What more could he break?' Matt asked anxiously.

'His back, Matt, his spine,' said Sam, almost in a whisper, his forehead all screwed up with worry.

Theo's head was cut and bruised, and blood was running out of the side of his mouth.

Caro wiped it away with his handkerchief. Her fingers were trembling.

'Sam, what's that? Is it dangerous?' she said.

'Probably only bitten his tongue,' said Sam firmly.

Theo's eyes were open but he did not seem to be looking at anything. His breathing sounded like gasping and sweat ran off his forehead.

'Give him some brandy,' said Madame. She had followed them in and was standing watching, leaning on her stick. 'In the dining-room.'

Matt ran to get the brandy, and then did not know which decanter it was in. Alix came to show him.

'Oh Matt,' she said. 'He's going to die, I know he is.'

'He isn't,' said Matt fiercely. He hurried back to the kitchen with the brandy.

Maggie poured some into a glass and gave it to Caro, who put her hand under Theo's head and held it to his lips. He drank a little but not much.

Nobody knew what to do. It was dreadful just to stand there and watch Theo, knowing he was in pain, and yet none of them could bear to go away and leave him. There was a sudden silence, and no sound but Theo's long, painful breaths.

Alix began to cry, not loudly, almost silently.

'It's my fault, it's my fault, oh, why did I go up on the roof?'

To everyone's surprise Madame spoke.

'No,' she said. 'It is my fault. Théo told me you would do something silly if I forbade you to come here. I did not believe him. Now he has killed himself over it.'

Alix hid her face on Maggie's shoulder, sobbing desolately.

Theo's eyes followed her gesture and he made an effort to speak.

'I'll be all right – soon – Alix,' he brought out at last, in a whisper.

A bell clanged outside and went on clanging.

'The ambulance is coming,' said Maggie with relief.

In a few moments the ambulance men were in the kitchen. It was not long before they had Theo on a stretcher and covered in a blanket, and carried him out to the ambulance. Sam climbed in after him and they drove off out of the gate, and everyone was left standing in the doorway feeling lost and uncertain what to do.

Caro gave a long sigh, and pushed back her hair, which was coming down.

'I suppose I had better get on with the supper,' she said in a flat tired voice and went back into the kitchen.

Alix was sitting on a stool, huddled up.

'When shall we know how he is?' she said.

'Sam will let us know,' said Maggie. 'He'll ring up or come back. Now, I think you had better have a little brandy, my dear. Just sip it slowly, very small sips.'

Madame had left the kitchen but Mademoiselle Tousselin came back to say, in a surprised voice, 'Mademoiselle Alix may have her supper here if she wishes, and wait for the news of Monsieur Théo.'

Alix stared in amazement.

'Gran'mère has given in,' she said.

'When it's too late,' said Caro bitterly.

'Madame will not dine, Miss Rendal,' said Mademoiselle. 'She will have a bowl of soup only, in her room. I will come and fetch it.'

'Thank you,' said Caro, mechanically.

Mademoiselle went away, sniffing sadly, and Maggie

took the children off upstairs. Bernadette was weeping desolately.

'Oh, Maggie,' she said. 'It did hurt him so much.'

Supper was a miserable and unwanted meal, nobody had the heart to eat much. Agnes stayed on even after the washing up was done, waiting for news of Theo.

Sam came back in a taxi about half-past nine. He still looked very tired and anxious, but he tried to speak cheerfully.

'They say he's got a good chance, as far as they can tell,' he said. 'He's broken a lot of bones, but not his spine, thank God. Dislocated things too, that's partly what was so painful. But they seem to think there's nothing really fatal, and that he's tough enough to survive it.'

'Thank God for that,' said Maggie. 'But will he get really better, Sam? He won't be crippled by it?'

'It's too soon to tell,' said Sam. 'We must hope for the best. Who's going to tell Mrs Ayre?'

'I will,' said Alix, getting up. She kissed Maggie and Caro good night, very quiet and subdued, and went away.

'Poor child, she must feel terrible,' said kind Maggie.

'And perhaps she should,' said Caro, rather sternly.

When Caro came to say good night to Matt he gave her a tight hug.

'Oh, Caro, how awful it was!'

She held him close, but did not say anything.

'Caro, what about his shoes?'

She looked round and saw them lying there, large muddy old shoes with the laces still done up, because he had pulled them off in such a hurry. Tears came into her eyes. She went and picked them up, and his socks, stuck with bits of hay, and his glove.

'Oh, Matt,' she said, as she went to the door. 'Pray hard for Theo.'

Matt lay in the dark and tried to stop thinking about Theo falling down into the yard, and to pray for him instead. In the middle of his prayers he fell fast asleep.

17

After the Accident

THE next morning Sam rang up the hospital and reported that Theo was expected to recover from his injuries in time; none of them were likely to prove fatal.

'They said he was comfortable,' said Sam. 'That means very uncomfortable, but not in real danger. If he was in danger they would say he was in a critical condition.'

'Why don't they tell the truth?' Matt said.

'All professions talk jargon,' said Sam. 'One has to pick it up as one goes along.'

Everyone missed Theo very much. It was surprising, in a way, how different Woodhall seemed without him, and surprising too how many jobs were not done because Theo usually did them. He never seemed to hurry or be at all busy, but in fact he had been doing things all day long.

In the evening Sam went to see Theo but when he came back he said, 'He was very dopey, not able to talk much. He sent his love to everyone.'

Two days later Matt had to go back to school and Caro got permission to take him to see Theo in the afternoon, as it was visiting day, on the way back to Birmingham. They walked along the shiny echoing passages with the other visitors, feeling untidy, bloated and dirty compared with the neatness and antiseptic cleanness of the hospital. Theo was at the end of a ward, and he looked much too long and too large for the narrow hospital bed, Matt thought. He was lying down and had a bandage round his head, his shrunken arm was done up in a splint, and there was something under the bedclothes to lift them off him, but out of all this his face looked at them, just the same, only rather bruised and black round the eyes.

'Hullo,' he said, smiling. 'How nice of you to come.'

'We've brought you some flowers and grapes,' said Matt, putting the grapes on the locker and the flowers, which were freesias, on top of Theo.

'What lovely things,' he said, touching them gently with his fingers, though he could hardly move his arm.

'How are you, Theo?' Caro asked, sitting down on the chair beside him.

'I feel like a chicken trussed for the oven,' he said. 'The doctors don't think much of me. I'm a very dull case, just multiple fractures and things. No interesting complications!' He smiled. 'How's Alix? I hope she isn't worrying too much?'

'She's very subdued,' said Caro.

'She sent her love, everyone did,' said Matt. 'Everybody says how much they miss you.'

'How nice of them,' said Theo. 'I miss you all too. We must scrape up some money to get the roofs mended, mustn't we? Woodhall mustn't fall to pieces if St Raphael's is going to be there. Are you going back to school, Matt?'

'Yes, worse luck.'

'Don't you like it?'

'School's all right,' said Matt. 'But really I don't like living with Aunt Maud, and I'm afraid she doesn't like it either.'

'Couldn't you be a weekly boarder?' Theo said.

'Too expensive,' said Caro briefly. She glanced round the ward. 'Are you all right here, Theo? What's it like?'

'It's all right, rather noisy,' said Theo. 'It's like living in a factory, a very clean factory of course. In fact, I feel very like a piece of machinery undergoing repairs: someone is always coming to check the functions! Not that the nurses aren't nice; they are, of course. But it's not very restful, except in the middle of the night. Time comes in snippets, otherwise.'

'Isn't it boring? Can't you read?' Matt asked.

'I haven't felt like reading yet,' said Theo. 'I've caught up on my rosary, though. He held up his hand with the beads wound round it. 'Haven't said so many for ages.'

'Say one for me,' Caro said.

'I've said lots for you,' said Theo smiling. 'And Matt. That's easy. It's cousin Jasper and characters like that who take a bit of doing.'

A nurse came and told them they must go.

'He shouldn't really be having visitors yet,' she said.

'Why not?' said Matt anxiously.

'They think I might bite them,' said Theo, with a smile. The nurse laughed.

'I'll put your flowers in water,' she said, picking them up. 'Aren't they lovely?'

She took them away and Caro said, 'I can see you're going to be everyone's favourite patient, Theo!'

'There's nothing like lying still and watching other people work, is there?' he said laughing.

Matt said good-bye. 'I shan't see you till half-term,' he said. 'I do hope you'll be better then, Theo.'

'Better! We'll all have forgotten about this by then,"' said Theo cheerfully.

They went away down the ward and looked back at the door to see Theo still watching them. He gave them a rather restricted wave with his free hand.

'What a good person he is,' said Caro as they went out

into the cold grey afternoon. 'I've never known anyone who made so little fuss, just taking things as they come.'

Matt went back to the spring term at school, to long cold weeks in loud and murky winter Birmingham, with Aunt Maud in a perpetual grumble over the mud Matt brought into her neat little house, and the number of times he tore his clothes.

'And now Caroline has broken her engagement to that charming and suitable young man,' she said. 'I can't think what possessed her to do such a thing.'

'She found she didn't love him after all,' said Matt.

Aunt Maud sniffed. 'It seems to me nobody is good enough for Miss Caroline,' she said. 'I really thought that this time there would be a home for you, Matthew, and a man's discipline, which is what you need.'

'Do I?' said Matt, surprised. He could not imagine Jasper being much use to him, or that he needed discipline, which he took to mean a kind of army regulation of his life.

'Caroline had better be careful,' said Aunt Maud. 'She's pretty enough, but good looks don't last for ever and she'll find herself a penniless spinster, one of these days.'

'Caro wouldn't mind,' said Matt. 'Miss Sonning is a penniless spinster and everyone seems to like her tremendously.'

Miss Sonning had come to Woodhall after Theo's accident, the day before Matt had left. She was tall and thin with a long nose and spectacles and yellowy-white hair done in a bun, and the children greeted her with cries of delight. At first sight Matt had thought she looked severe, but when she smiled he realized why the children liked her. Her eyes twinkled like a naughty little girl's as she gave Mickey a joke matchbox, which he loved. She had little things for them all.

But Aunt Maud was not at all interested in Miss Sonning, or St Raphael's, or Woodhall. Nor was Tunstall, at school. 'It sounds a daft place,' he said, bored. 'Why don't they give it to the National Trust?'

It was one of the trials of life in Birmingham that there was no one Matt could talk to about Woodhall. He made a calendar with coloured circles for days and crossed them out towards half-term. But before he reached it he got 'flu, which annoyed Aunt Maud and upset Matt because he had to miss his holiday. His only comfort was that Caro wrote to say he was not missing much, as Alix was in bed with a cold and Theo was still in the hospital. Even Madame was not very well and had taken to her bed.

'Life seems to be all trays,' she said.

Matt lay in bed feeling unwell and fed up with Birmingham, and perhaps because he was alone and ill himself he began to worry about Theo. Why was he still in hospital after all this time? He had said they would have forgotten all about the accident by half-term. Matt could not help remembering what Maggie had said, asking Sam if Theo would be crippled by his fall, and Sam had said it was too soon to tell. Suppose they had found out by now that he would never get really better, would always be ill, or have to go about in a wheelchair like Mickey? It was a dreadful thought to Matt. It seemed to him that it was bad enough for Theo not to have two hands like everyone else. Besides, he was such an active person, always doing things. Matt thought of him cutting down the pine tree for Christmas, and riding on Nero up by Bertrand's Tower. At last he could bear it no longer. He decided to write to Theo himself and ask him. 'He'll tell me,' he thought.

He had a feeling that Caro would not tell him the worst, because she knew he liked Theo so much. So he wrote his letter and Aunt Maud posted it, and then he had to wait for the answer,

It came quite soon. Theo had written in pencil.

'My Biro has rolled under the bed,' he wrote. 'Why doesn't someone invent a square pen that doesn't roll? My writing is so bad because I'm holding the pad up in the air, not because I am at death's door. I'm sorry you have been worrying about me, Matt, because I'm really much better. It's just that bones take so long to grow together again, I didn't realize how long, myself. I managed to break the big bone in my thigh, and the little bone in my shin as well, besides all those stupid ribs, what a lot one seems to have. The doctors think it was a miracle they didn't puncture my lungs or anything equally unpleasant and keep telling me how lucky I am, so I expect my guardian angel arranged the way I fell and perhaps St Raphael as well. Anyway, it's all going to mend all right in the end, they say, and they're doing all sorts of things to make sure my leg doesn't finish up shorter than the other, so you see there is nothing to worry about. Get better yourself as quick as you can and we'll both be back at Woodhall for the holidays.'

Matt was so relieved that he at once felt better himself, and made a good recovery from the 'flu. All the same it seemed a very long time before the end of term. He heard from Caro, before then, that Theo had come home, but had to lie down a lot of the time; Matt couldn't imagine him doing that. She mentioned, too, that Madame was in bed again, not well. Her letters were hurried, and did not tell him much.

The March day was chilly and bright, clouds streaming

over a high blue sky, when Matt at last arrived in Bewdley. It was Price who met him and Price who actually answered, though briefly, his questions.

'Yes, Mr Ayre is back at last,' he said. 'That was a pity it was my day off, when he went on the roof. No business to go climbing, a one-armed man.'

'Lucky for Alix he did,' said Matt.

'Ah,' said Price. 'Put a little sense in her, that has.'

'How's Madame?'

'It's all too much excitement for the old lady,' said Price. 'But that made her think, Mr Ayre falling like that. Saw what it would be like without him, maybe. Can't tell, with a queer case like that.'

Matt was astonished and still more so when after a long pause Price added, 'Maybe her Rosario's been busy in heaven.'

After that he relapsed into his usual silence.

Theo was actually in the yard when they drove into it, talking to Alix, who had just come in on Primrose, her pony. Matt was pleased to see him standing up again. He looked thinner than before his fall and was leaning on a walking-stick; otherwise he was just the same.

Matt tumbled out of the car and Alix jumped off Primrose, delighted to see him again. She ran up and gave him a kiss, which rather startled him. Theo shook hands with him and Caro came running out and gave him a hug.

'Come in and get warm,' she said, and turned to Theo. 'Will you stay and have tea with us?' she asked, quite shyly and anxiously, as if he might refuse.

'Well, thank you very much,' he said, but not without hesitation.

Matt was surprised, and wondered if they had been going on in this formal way ever since the disastrous tea-party which Madame had brought to such an uncomfortable end.

'Oh Theo, you're lame!' he cried, startled and alarmed when he saw Theo move, limping unevenly along with his stick.

Theo laughed. 'All right, all right,' he said. 'Don't tell me I'm a liar! I'm not crippled for life, Matt, I assure you.'

'The doctors think he's doing very well,' said Alix. 'They didn't expect him to get about so soon.'

'I was determined to get home,' said Theo, but he sat down thankfully all the same, in the armchair at the end of the table. 'But I'm afraid I'm not a very useful inhabitant yet, hardly earning my oats.'

'We like giving you your oats free,' said Alix affectionately. 'Have some free toast, I made it myself.' She seemed, now, much more at home in the kitchen than he was.

Alix and Matt did most of the talking. Caro just smiled and poured out tea and Theo sat and drank it, and laughed at Alix's nonsense, but did not say much himself. After tea he said he must go and see his mother and limped slowly away, pushing the baize door open with his stick.

When Matt was in bed that night and Caro came to tuck him in, he asked her, 'Why were you and Theo behaving as if you hardly knew each other?'

'Were we?' said Caro. 'Well, perhaps we don't. He never just comes in like he used to. If I don't ask him I don't believe he would at all.'

'How peculiar,' said Matt.

Caro sighed. 'I expect it's because I said those stupid things about not intending to entangle him in my wiles,' she said. 'And saying I never asked him to come. I could kick myself for that, it wasn't fair to someone like him.'

'Why not?'

'Because he's much too humble he took it literally,' said Caro. 'Jasper would have got cross or sulky, but Theo evidently thought it was just a way of showing how little I cared about him. It must have sounded very scornful, as if it wasn't even worth being polite to him.'

'So then you didn't really mean it?' Matt said.

'Of course not,' said Caro. 'I was cross, because Madame made me sound so calculating and horrid, and I didn't want Theo to think I was like that. I never realized how much he would mind.'

'Madame went on about it to him afterwards,' said Matt. 'She said he hadn't enough money to make it worth while for you to marry someone who had an arm like that.'

'Oh dear,' said Caro. 'What did he say?' She seemed very anxious.

'He didn't say anything,' said Matt. 'He was trying to talk to her about Alix. But do you mind his arm, Caro?'

'Of course I don't mind it,' Caro said. 'How could she say a thing like that? I believe it annoys her when she sees how people like him, it makes her feel guilty because she has been so unfair to him herself.'

'So you do like him, don't you, Caro?' said Matt.

Caro did not answer this directly. She said thoughtfully, 'You know, Matt, when I first met Theo I thought he was rather a weak person, a passive character, because he let people say what they liked about him and didn't seem to have any authority in his own house. It was awfully stupid of me.'

'You don't think that now, then?' said Matt.

'I should say not!' said Caro. She was sitting on his bed, clasping her hands round her knees, her face a little

179

flushed, her eyes very bright. 'I think he's one of the strongest people I know, strong in an enduring kind of way, without pushing himself to the front all the time or ordering people about and interfering with them, or trying to make them do what he wants, unless it's something that must be done. And when I think what a lonely difficult life he's had I'm all the more surprised. Most people would have turned sour and bitter and tried to get their own back, but he's always ready to give anyone anything he can, and do anything for them, whether it's a big thing or a little thing.'

'Well!' said Matt, astonished. 'I didn't know you thought he was as wonderful as all that!'

Caro went very red and laughed and jumped up and kissed him. 'No,' she said. 'I didn't know myself till I thought he was killed, that dreadful night. Now go to sleep, Matt darling, it's lovely to have you back.'

18

A Way for Madame

THE Sunday after Matt's return was Passion Sunday. He discovered that Theo had got permission for mass to be said regularly in the chapel, because of the difficulty of transporting the children to the church. Priests came over from a seminary not far away.

Theo was determined to have all the St Raphael's children there, and was planning how to use the rooms upstairs to the best advantage. He had persuaded Sam to stop looking for another house.

'But what does Madame say?' Matt asked, when he heard all this after mass.

'She says nothing about it, one way or the other,' said Theo.

It was Madame's birthday that day and Matt found that, unknown to Theo, the children had made her a present. It was Bernadette's idea, a tray-cloth on which each child had embroidered a flower, though Noel's, and some of the others', were really done by Maggie, who was the only grown-up in the secret.

It was to be given to Madame when her tea was taken in, and as it was Sunday Caro was taking it, and Matt went too, to carry the cake. Madame's bedroom was very big and full of furniture. Not only were Alix and Mademoiselle there to have tea with her, but Theo as well, looking very clean and neat in the suit he had worn before to impress Sir Godfrey. Madame was sitting up against a pile of lace-edged pillows, wearing a lavender-coloured bed-jacket, with a pretty shawl over her head and shoulders. Even in bed she looked very trim and regal, and sat upright, her eyes as black and sharp as ever.

Caro laid the table with the best cloth and china and Matt handed her the things from his tray.

Then came the presentation. Bernadette came in, shepherding the smallest of the girls, who had a big built-up boot but otherwise was a normal and rather pretty child. Bernadette, who knew Madame's horror of deformity, kept her artificial hand behind her back.

'Please, Mrs Ayre,' she said. 'We heard it was your birthday and we have made you a present, because you are Theo's mother, and it's so kind of you to let us live in your house.'

She pushed the little girl forward, and she walked, with her jerky stumping gait, straight up to Madame's bed and held up the tray-cloth.

'Many Happy Returns of the Day from us St Raphael's children,' she repeated in a piping sing-song.

Madame took the cloth and spread it out and looked at it for a long moment in silence.

'Do you like it?' said the little girl, who hardly knew Madame and was not at all frightened of her. 'We all did a flower. That's mine.' She pointed with a stubby finger. 'I did a rose because my name is Rose.'

Madame gazed at her.

'What is your name?' she said at last, in a queer voice.

'Mary Rose,' said the child. 'I'm a rosary baby, that's what Mum – what Maggie calls me.'

'How old are you?'

'I'm seven.'

There was another long moment of silence. Then Madame said, 'I like your gift very much, little Rose.

Please thank all the other children. It was charming of you
to remember an old lady.'

'Oh, I'm glad you like it,' said Rose. 'It will do for
your breakfast tray, won't it?' Then she said, 'I think
your shawl is ever so pretty.'

'That is a present too, from Théo,' said Madame.

'Come along now, Rose,' said Bernadette.

'Wait,' said Madame. 'Rose must have some cake. Cut
her a piece of cake, Théo.'

'Oh, but you ought to cut it,' said Rose. 'It's your
birthday.'

'Very well. Théo shall bring it here.'

'Why do you call him Théo, and not Theo like us?'
Rose asked.

'Because I was born in France, little Rose, and that is
how we say it there.'

'France is where St Bernadette lived, Bernadette's own
saint,' said Rose. 'She saw our Lady in the rocks by the
river, didn't she?'

Everyone in the room but Rose was silent, in sheer
astonishment. But the little girl was not at all shy, chattered away, directed the cake-cutting, ate her own piece
with relish and finally went off carrying a plateful for the
other children. Caro and Matt followed her and Bernadette
out.

'Well!' said Caro. 'Who would have thought it?'

The two children went upstairs and Matt said to Caro,
'Madame's voice sounded quite quiet, quite different.'

'And yet, when Rose said her name I was afraid it
would have a dreadful effect,' said Caro. 'I think Theo
did too. He went quite white.'

Everyone was very surprised at the way Madame had
behaved on her birthday, and even more so when, the

next day, she asked for Rose to go and see her. Then, for a little while, Rose went every day and chattered to her and poked about among her things and never realized that other people were frightened of 'the France lady' as she called her. But she could not stay very long on her visits, for Madame was not well and tired easily. She spent long hours leaning back on her pillows, silent and open-eyed, gazing out of her window. Alix said that from it she could see the fountain in the Rose Round.

On the Friday of Passion Week Dom Richard Houghton arrived to spend Easter with them.

'Don't they need him in the monastery?' Matt said to Theo.

'There's a special reason for this,' Theo said gravely. 'We must all pray for my mother. I think she is dying.'

'Dying?' said Matt, surprised. 'But she doesn't seem very ill.'

'She is getting weaker and weaker,' said Theo. 'All this time she has been so active and strong, but since my accident in January she has given up all her interests. You must pray for her, please Matt. We want Dom Richard to bring her back to God before she leaves this life.'

'But now that she's just beginning to be nice to the children she ought not to die,' Matt said.

'St Raphael has sent her another little Rose to make the way easier for her,' said Theo.

Afterwards Matt said to Caro, 'But after all, I don't see why it should be made easier for her. She's made things very hard for everyone else, especially Theo.'

'Yes, I suppose we're bound to feel like that,' said Caro. 'But we mustn't be like the elder brother in the story, who was jealous because his father welcomed back his bad young brother. The important thing is that old

Mrs Ayre should be sorry, not whether she suffers for her unkindness.'

All through Holy Week everyone prayed for Mrs Ayre, though she did not know it. Dom Richard visited her every day, and now the doctor was coming too. Suddenly everyone seemed to know she was dying.

'She's failing,' said Agnes.

Price said, 'That kind goes quickly at the end.'

No one was very sad, though it seemed to make everyone solemn. Matt wondered if anybody really loved the hard, selfish old woman. Even her friend, Sir Godfrey Hartnoll, though he called to see her, seemed to take her going for granted and was not particularly upset by it.

'She's had wonderful health all her life,' Matt heard him say as he came out of the front door with Theo. Matt was hiding under the laurels, having a look at the Daimler without letting Sir Godfrey's chauffeur see him.

'And how are you now, Theo?' Sir Godfrey went on, looking at Theo, who was back in his ordinary untidy state. 'I didn't expect to see you on your feet yet.'

'The doctors say I was lucky,' said Theo. 'The ladder broke my fall, in spite of being such an uncomfortable thing to fall on.'

'I suppose you'll have to sell the place when poor Louise is gone?' said Sir Godfrey.

'No, I'll have the school here,' said Theo.

'Madness!' said Sir Godfrey. 'Take on a charitable institution with no responsible backing? You'll be penniless in a year.'

'I'm pretty well penniless now,' said Theo cheerfully. 'St Raphael will look after us. He always has, so far.'

'Ridiculous nonsense!' said Sir Godfrey, huffily, and got into his Daimler.

On Easter morning, after mass, when Caro and Matt were finishing their breakfast, Theo looked round the door.

'May I come in?'

He came in and they saw he was smiling.

'I just wanted to tell you it's all right,' he said. 'Mamma is making her confession to Dom Richard now. When I went to see her after mass she said, "It's Easter and I had better make my duties," just like that.'

'Oh, I am glad,' said Caro. 'That makes this a specially happy Easter Day. I wonder what finally brought her to do it?'

'She had a photograph in her hand,' said Theo. 'Rosario in her First Communion dress. Perhaps she realized at last that the way not to lose her was to share her with God, and God with her. Anyway, she's done it.'

'Is she sorry now, then?' Matt said.

'Yes,' said Theo.

'Did she say sorry to you too?' Matt said.

'That doesn't matter,' said Theo.

Although he tried, Matt could not feel as happy as he ought to feel. He could not help thinking that Madame had got off very lightly. It was only when he once passed the door and saw Madame's tired old face that he felt a little sorry for her. 'After all,' he thought, 'she's made herself very unhappy all this time.'

And he heard her murmuring, 'I have wasted my life, I have wasted my life.'

Perhaps it was a pain to her to feel that, a punishment to know that she had so long rejected love, the only life that survives death. It occurred to Matt that purgatory must be like that.

Madame repeated those words very often in the next

few days. Everyone passing her room heard the old voice murmuring that lament, sometimes in English, more often in French.

'I have wasted my life.'

She grew weaker and weaker every day. Everyone knew she was going to die, everyone was waiting for her to die.

One evening Caro had taken in a hot drink to her and came back to the kitchen looking grave and quiet, somehow both sad and happy at the same time.

'Matt,' she said. 'Theo was there and they did not see me come in. The door was open. Madame had her hand on Theo's bad hand and she said to him, 'Theo, I am ashamed.'

'And what did he do?' Matt said.

'He kissed her,' said Caro.

Louise Ayre died the next day, quietly, having received the Last Sacraments.

19

The Hours are Counted

So Mrs Ayre was gone, her requiem said, and prayers
followed her into the world beyond time. And when she
was gone, Woodhall was changed. Now anyone could go
anywhere in the house, the children played on the lawn,
and the school dining-room and the bedrooms of those
who found stairs difficult were moved to the ground floor.
Sam and Maggie were very busy getting ready for the rest
of the children, who were to come at the end of April.

Theo was not so busy. He would have liked to have
been, but the doctor told him he was doing too much too
soon and must rest more if he really wanted to get strong
again and not be lame always. It seemed strange to see
him lying about on sofas, and in fact he often forgot to
do what he was told.

Not long after Madame's death, Matt, looking for his
sister, found her in her room, crying on her bed. She was
crying so hard she could not pretend she wasn't; her face
was all red and wet with tears.

'Oh, Caro!' said Matt, horrified and worried. 'What's
the matter?'

'Oh dear!' she gasped. 'Oh dear! I went to see Theo
and said I supposed now that Madame was gone he
wouldn't need another cook for the school, and – and he
– said, no, he wouldn't!'

Matt was aghast. 'Does that mean we've got to go?'
he said,

'Yes, it does,' said Caro, with a sob. She rubbed her

face with a wet handkerchief. 'I was so afraid I'd burst out howling I rushed away without asking him when, or anything.'

'Shall I ask him?' Matt said.

'No, no, don't say anything. Leave it to him,' said Caro. 'Let's stay here as long as we can.'

Matt said, 'It's very surprising, considering Theo's in love with you.'

'Oh, don't be silly!' said Caro, fiercely. ' Just because of something he said to you long ago last summer, before everything happened!'

She would not listen any more, and Matt wondered if perhaps she was right. People seemed to fall out of love as well as in, as Caro herself had with Jasper. Perhaps Theo did not feel the same now as he had before. Matt would have liked to ask him and make sure, but he did not get the chance. Wherever Theo was, even when he lay down to rest, he was immediately surrounded by people, especially the children, and very often he had Noel with him, showing him picture books or telling him stories, to pass the time for both of them. Now the once empty rooms of Woodhall echoed with children's noise; although there were only eleven, counting Matt and Alix, the house seemed alive with them. But still Theo never went into Caro's kitchen, and now she did not ask him.

One bright April day Matt and Alix went into the woods, and spent most of the morning patching up their house in the tree. The worst of this tree house was that when it was finished there was nothing much that could be done with it. The fun was all in the making. There was just room for them both to sit in it, either with their legs curled under or hanging outside, but they soon got tired of this and climbed down. The weather was still showery and the brambles in the wood were all dewed with drops, bright as crystals in the sharp spring sunlight. It was sunny even in the wood, because the leaves were not yet thick; some trees were bare rods still, some tightly budded, some showing soft new curling fronds of leaf.

They walked under the pines and heard again that soft sighing, the breathing of earth, so like the sea, the whisper that called away the heart to mysterious regions where anything might happen.

They listened, walking under the tall red masts of the pines, with their crust of ornate brocaded bark, looking up at the swaying boughs, blue-green always, alive all the year round with their fringes of stiff needles, and it was because the needles were so stiff that the wind made this strange sound, blowing through.

They walked on, among other trees now, oak and ash and hazel, and came out by the path that joined the ride where Bertrand's Tower stood, white in the strong noonday sun.

Theo was coming up the slope on Nero's back. The black horse saw the children, but this time he did not shy.

Theo drew rein, and dismounted, slowly and awkwardly.

'I'm sure you ought not to be riding,' said Alix. 'I'll tell Dr Stirling how wicked you are.'

'It's easier than walking, except for getting on and off,' said Theo.

'Why do either?' Matt said.

'I came up here to find something I think I must have left in the tower in the winter,' said Theo.

'What?' asked Alix.

Theo laughed. 'Aren't you inquisitive? Why should I tell you?'

'We could help you to find it,' said Matt.

'No, thank you,' said Theo. He hitched Nero's reins round one of the pillars and went into the tower.

Alix and Matt stood outside.

'Let's go after him,' said Alix.

'Perhaps he doesn't want us to,' said Matt.

'He didn't say so,' said Alix and she went up the steps and in at the door, so of course Matt went after her.

Theo was already half-way up the narrow stair, which he was finding difficult to negotiate. He climbed out, panting, into the room with the celestial globe, and Alix and Matt skipped up the stairs behind him, just in time to see him pick up a dusty piece of paper from the window-sill and put it in his pocket.

'Was that what you came for?' Alix asked.

'Yes,' said Theo, smiling at her. 'Beat you to it, Miss Alix.'

'What is it? Do tell me,' she coaxed.

'It looked like poetry,' said sharp-eyed Matt.

'Let's go on the roof,' said Theo quickly, starting up the wooden ladder.

'I'm sure it's bad for your bones to climb all these stairs,' said Alix. 'Not to mention the muscles that got torn out, or whatever it was.'

'They're all right now, really,' said Theo. He squeezed through the little door on to the roof and they followed him.

It was windy and sunny up there. The shade of the gnomon on the sundial pointed exactly at the figure twelve.

'Noon,' said Theo, breathlessly, finding a muddy-looking handkerchief and then wiping the sweat from his face with his sleeve.

'Theo,' said Matt. 'What does that mean: PEREUNT ET IMPUTANTUR?'

Theo leant against the parapet. The wind blew his untidy dark hair on end.

'It means "They perish and are counted up,"' he said, and sighed.

'What perish and are counted?'

'The hours,' said Theo. 'The days, all our time, our times, our journeys round the sun.'

Alix said, 'I don't like that motto.'

'They do perish, though,' said Theo. 'We can't bring back what has gone.'

'Counted,' said Matt. 'Who counts them?'

'They are counted,' said Theo. 'Not necessarily against us.'

'It's the perishing I don't like,' said Alix. 'It's awful to think this minute's gone, and now this minute, and will never come back. Then one day there won't be any minutes left, not one.'

'Then we shall go out of time altogether,' said Theo. 'Time is only the way we know things here; it's not the only way to know them. It will be different in the eternal world.'

'I don't like the word eternal,' said Alix. 'It's so huge and hollow-sounding, and unreal.'

'But there was nothing unreal about Christ when he rose from the grave,' said Theo. 'It was time and space, walls and moments that were unreal; he just walked through them.'

'It's an upside-down world,' Matt said. He thought of that because he was looking in a puddle on the roof and saw there the sky upside down, like a pale shadowy sea, and the trees growing head down, bare waving weeds.

'This is the world that's upside down,' said Theo. He leant his elbow on the parapet and looked away to the house, sedate and red, sitting in its green lawns, in the middle of the woods.

'Look, the children are playing ball on the lawn, with Sam,' said Alix.

Their figures, in a wide circle, were tiny far away, like another sundial, Matt thought, only these figures moved. Then Alix said it.

'They're like a sundial too.'

'Games played in circles are games of the sun,' said Theo.

'Ring of roses,' said Matt. 'The Rose Round.'

He could see the Rose Round from here, away in its corner by the woods, and suddenly remembered looking through the telescope at it.

'We all go round the sun,' said Alix.

'And the sun is the shadow of God,' said Theo. 'LUX UMBRA DEI.'

'I like that better than perishing and being counted,' said Alix.

'Both are true,' said Theo. He stood up. 'I'm going back now, I don't know about you.'

Matt said suddenly, 'Theo, have we got to go? Caro and me?'

Theo looked down at him with troubled eyes.

'I can't keep you here, can I?' he said. 'She must go if she wants to go.'

'Can't she be another cook for the school?' Matt asked.

'No,' said Theo abruptly, and started squeezing through the little door to the wooden ladder.

He had never said 'No' so roughly to Matt before; it was a nasty shock and made his throat feel tight and his stomach hollow. He came to the top of the ladder, watching Theo slowly descending it. He felt very unhappy suddenly. When Theo got down to the floor he turned and looked up at Matt and saw at once that something was wrong.

'What's the matter, Matt?' he said, in his usual voice.

'Don't you want us here any more?' Matt said.

Theo said, 'I want you here more than anything in the world, but not like that. I don't want Caro here as a cook to the school, Matt, you know that. I told you long ago.'

'Wouldn't it be better than nothing?' Matt said hopefully.

'No,' said Theo, but quite quietly this time. He turned away and began going down the narrow stairs, holding the wall to steady himself. 'It would be much worse.'

'What are you doing, Matt?' Alix said impatiently. She was stuck on the roof still, because he was in the doorway.

Matt came down to the room where the globe was, and Alix ran down the ladder and skipped across and passed him.

'Are you all right, Uncle Theo?' she said going down behind him.

Ever since the accident she had shown herself much more fond of him, and anxious to help.

Matt stood in the dim room with its twelve slits of window, and the great yellow globe of the heavens in the middle. He felt sure now that Theo had not changed, he still wanted to marry Caro, but he thought she did not care, and only wanted to stay to help with the school. Matt put his hand on the globe and swung it slowly over.

'I'm turning the whole sky over and all the stars,' he thought, watching the shadowy figures of the constellations as they turned.

Then he went down the stairs after the others and caught them up in the portico. Theo was unhitching Nero's reins.

'Give me a leg-up, Matt, will you?' he said.

When he was up Alix said, 'We can't go as fast as Nero.'

'I'm not waiting for you,' said Theo, with a smile, and he rode away down the green hill.

'Ha ha!' said Alix mischievously. 'I'm glad he went off like that!' She pulled out of her pocket the piece of paper Theo had picked up from the window-sill.

'Alix! How did you get that?'

'Pinched it, coming down the stairs. I saw it sticking out of his pocket. He really is terribly careless.'

They put their heads together over it.

'It *is* a poem,' said Matt.

It was in Theo's crabbed left-handed writing, full of crossings-out and unfinished. 'I believe he's written it himself.'

'Well, it's written to someone else then,' said Alix. 'It says 'you' several times. Oh Matt, I believe it's a love poem, how funny!'

Matt had just guessed the same thing, and quicker than Alix he guessed for whom it was written. He grabbed it.

'Hey! What are you doing?' Alix cried.

'I know who it's for and I'm going to give it to her.'

'Why? Is it Caro?'

'Yes,' said Matt. 'And she thinks he doesn't love her, so now I can prove it.'

'Does she love him?' said Alix, interested.

'I'm not waiting for you,' said Theo.

'I don't know,' said Matt. 'She seems to admire him a lot, and she was crying like anything at the idea of going away.'

'Oh, wouldn't it be fun if they got married?' said Alix, delighted. 'What relation should we be then, Matt? Theo's my uncle and Caro's your sister, does that make you my uncle? Ha ha! Uncle Matt, how funny!'

'They aren't married yet,' Matt reminded her. 'And they don't look like bringing it off, either. They never go near each other now.'

They discussed the problem all the way back to the house. Alix was full of such hair-raising and impossible plans that Matt wished she knew nothing about it. But in the end she agreed there was nothing to be done except to show Caro the unfinished poem. Matt did that at lunch time, when they were alone in the kitchen.

Caro read it over and over, without saying anything, several times.

'Can you understand it?' Matt said. 'It looks an awful muddle to me. I'm sure half the lines don't scan.'

'I understand what he means,' said Caro softly.

She would not say any more.

20

East Gate of Spring

AFTER the showery morning it was a sunny, clear afternoon. The wind dropped and the sky was very high and blue. Alix was having a music lesson with Mr Howell and through the open windows the sound of the harp fell in long runs of wiry gold down into the bright air. It reminded Matt of the fountain in the Rose Round and he went wandering that way to look at it, for Price had turned on the water again at Easter. It was pleasant to be able to go through the garden of Woodhall freely, and not feel the house was the home of watching, hostile eyes.

Matt went slowly, meandering along a path where daffodils grew on the strip of rough grass each side, and hyacinths white and crimson, stiff and curled. He came to the yew hedge, so dark and thick, and went through the gap. And there he stopped, staring, for in the middle of the Rose Round by the fountain Theo and Caro were standing, close in each other's arms, and they were kissing. Caro was standing on the step of the fountain, to reach him better.

Although he thought he knew all about it, Matt was quite surprised now that it had happened, and he stood still, gaping. Neither of them noticed him at first, but just as he was wondering if he ought to go away, Theo saw him.

'There's Matt,' he said.

Caro turned her head.

'Oh Matt, darling!' she said, smiling with happiness. 'Everything's all right now.'

'Are you going to marry Theo, then?' he said, going towards them.

'Yes, I am.'

'Thank goodness you didn't marry Jasper,' said Matt earnestly.

'Thank goodness indeed!' said Theo, laughing. 'But I can hardly believe yet that she is going to marry me.'

'I practically had to ask him myself!' Caro said, laughing too and looking round at Theo. 'He was dreadfully suspicious of me, at first! I believe he thought I was teasing him, because of that poem you showed me, Matt.'

'Really, Matt, are you in training to be a great detective?' said Theo. But he was smiling, not annoyed at all. 'But I'm very glad to hear you've been on my side all the time.'

'So has Caro really,' said Matt.

'That's perfectly true,' said Caro. 'But I took much too long to realize it!'

'I don't believe you were on my side the day I knocked Jasper down,' said Theo.

'Yes, I was,' said Caro. 'I was shocked at myself for feeling just a little bit pleased, that's why I was so cross about it.'

'I wish I'd known that then,' said Theo.

'I'm not sure I knew it myself,' said Caro.

They began to laugh again.

'You are laughing a lot,' Matt said.

'It's because we're happy,' said Caro. 'There's the school tea-bell.'

They walked back to the house all together, and Alix met them, skipping across the lawn, and had to be told the news. She was wildly excited.

'When will you be married? May I be bridesmaid?'

'Goodness, we haven't thought of that yet!' said Caro.

'She'll make an enchanting bridesmaid for you,' said Theo. 'Because she's dark and you are so fair.'

'I'd like to have Bernadette as well,' said Caro.

'She'd love that,' Theo said. He was walking with his arm round Caro, and now he suddenly gave her a little kiss on the side of her head. 'It was a very nice idea,' he said.

They went into the house to tea, and after that it was all congratulations and everybody kissing everybody and all talking at once.

It was not till Caro came to say good night to Matt that he saw her alone.

'Caro,' he said, 'you won't break off your engagement to Theo, will you?'

She laughed. 'No, of course not. I love him much too much.'

'More than you did Jasper?'

'Darling Matt, it's quite different.'

'How, different?' he asked.

'I realize now I didn't really love Jasper at all,' said Caro. 'I just thought it would be suitable if I did.'

'How do you know it's different with Theo?'

'It just is,' she said. 'I'd do anything for him, go to the North Pole if he wanted to. I can't bear to think of being anywhere without him. Goodness, I am lucky to have found someone like him!'

She seemed perfectly sure, so Matt's last doubts vanished.

The next day Theo talked to him about Aunt Maud and suggested he should be a weekly boarder at school and come back to Woodhall at week-ends.

'But it's too expensive,' Matt said.

'I think we can manage that all right,' said Theo,

smiling. 'Otherwise we shouldn't see nearly enough of you. I'm going to send Alix to school, to see if the nuns can put some sense into her, and I hope we can make her a week-ender too.'

'But I thought Sir Godfrey said you had no money at all, Theo,' said Matt, worried.

Theo laughed. 'He means compared with him,' he said. 'I have some from my mother now. It isn't a great deal, but it will cover your school bills! Whether we can keep our own school going here is another question. But I've got a feeling St Raphael always had his eye on this house for us!'

But Matt was frowning, still not quite satisfied.

'I don't see why you should pay for me to go to school, Theo,' he said.

'Why not? You're going to be my brother now,' said Theo, and smiled. 'If you don't mind having such an aged brother!'

'Not your real brother,' said Matt.

They were in the Library, the only place where there was a chance of talking to Theo alone without being interrupted. Now Theo looked at him for a moment in silence and then he said seriously, 'You know, Matt, I wasn't very good friends with my real brother. He despised me and hated being younger than I was, and I'm afraid sometimes I hated him for always getting the better of me.'

'Did you really, Theo?' said Matt. 'Did you fight then?'

'You don't need to fight people to hate them,' said Theo. 'In fact, you often fight more with your friends than your enemies.'

This was true, Matt knew, from his own experience with Tunstall and the others at school

'I knew I ought not to hate him,' said Theo, 'but it

was very difficult not to, especially as if I said I was sorry he only laughed at me. I did try not to, but it kept coming back at me till I could get away and make my own life, and then, you see, he was killed in the war, so we never made friends. It doesn't make me happy to think of him, because I failed there so badly.'

'I don't see how you can like people who are beastly to you,' said Matt, thinking how Julian Ayre used to get a gang of friends to tease Theo, and shut him in the cellar, and laugh at him.

'Perhaps you can't like them,' said Theo. 'But you ought not to hate them, to keep on thinking about what they have done to you, and wish something nasty would happen to them. If you go on like that in the end you get to the point where you would hate it if they were sorry, because you would rather have the excuse to go on hating them.'

'But you didn't do that, Theo,' said Matt. 'You aren't like that.'

'I might have been,' said Theo, 'if it hadn't been for Sam and Maggie.'

'How did Sam help?' Matt asked.

'He gave me something to do that was worth doing,' said Theo, 'and made me see I could do it if I tried. It was easier then to forget how unhappy I had been here. I was Sam's first cripple, Matt, a grown-up one!' He smiled and went on, 'I'm telling you all this to show you how much I should like to feel you are my brother, because you're Caro's, and I want to share everything with her, and we get on all right, don't we? But of course,' and he began to laugh, 'of course you may think it's just funny having such an old brother.'

'No, I don't,' said Matt at once. 'And I always did

think Julian sounded awful, only I can't say so to Alix of course.'

'It wasn't only Julian's fault,' said Theo.

'No, it was Madame's,' said Matt.

'Mine too,' said Theo. 'If I had learned sooner that we can't control anyone's feelings but our own, it wouldn't have been so bad.'

'But can you?' Matt said. 'Feelings just seem to come, somehow.'

'Yes, they do just come,' said Theo. 'But you can do quite a lot about them when they are there. If you ever feel miserable and furious because of what someone's said to you, just try it and see. Say to yourself, "I can't do anything about him, but I can do something about myself, and I'm not going to let all that go on worrying me."'

Matt was silent, thinking about it, and Theo was silent, looking out of the window at the sunny green world outside, and perhaps at Bertrand's Tower up on the ridge, where he had gone so often to struggle alone with his troubles, and yet not alone because the maker of stars and men was always there.

'Well,' said Theo at last, 'all that's over now and everything's beginning again. Here's you and Alix and all the children at Woodhall, and Caro saying she loves me, which I can hardly believe yet! Nothing to worry about any more.'

'All the same, I don't want to be a nuisance,' said Matt.

'Nuisance! Good heavens,' said Theo. 'I don't believe I'd have got my Caro at all if it hadn't been for you!'

It seemed funny to hear him say 'my Caro,' but Matt suddenly liked it. He realized how different everything was going to be, and that he was going to be part of

Theo's family now for always, and he was beginning to be excited about it. But he did not show it at once.

'Jasper thought I was a nuisance,' he said cautiously.

'Jasper! Who cares about Jasper?' said Theo light-heartedly. 'He's a first-class nuisance himself. We don't have to bother what he thinks any more.'

So this and many other things were settled in the next few days, including the date of the wedding, which was to be at mid-summer.

'The roses will be out then,' said Matt.

'And we'll put the statue of Our Lady back in the middle of them,' said Theo.

The morning that he was to go back to Birmingham and school, Matt got up very early and went downstairs quietly, through the empty, warm, silent kitchen, and out into the yard. The air was fresh and grey; it was not yet fully light. He was going to the Rose Round, but he was going the old way, through the wood. The trees stood up in a faint, cold mist, and silent, for there was no wind. Leaves were unfolding now on all the boughs and on the ground among last year's dead leaves primroses stuck up their pale unique faces, a yellow like no other yellow, almost in this dim light, green, small ghosts of the sun growing out of the earth, shadows, images of his circle of light, and yet each itself, single and alive.

Matt went on, and came to the mossy, ivy-twisted oak where he had built the tree house with Alix, and she had once annoyed him with her heartless words about Theo. When he had first met her Matt had thought she behaved like a princess in a fairy tale, proud and cool; no wonder, living alone in that great empty house with old Madame, so hard and cold in her extreme of pride and anger, Madame who had wasted her life because she could not have what she wanted, and would not give up her will to have it even when death had made it impossible. But now Alix had found her heart, perhaps a wild one, but certainly warm. Even Madame had thawed enough to go out of this world sorry for the pain she had caused in it.

'All that's over at last,' Matt said to himself, echoing what Theo had said. 'Now something new is beginning.'

He came to the old blue door and found that it had been rehung and opened quite easily. He went through and into the garden. Dew was on the daffodils and on the small leaves of box, or was it mist, turned to drops like diamonds? Here was the yew hedge, dark and thick, a wall you could not see through, always green, but with the ever-lasting green that reminds us more of time than the leaves that fall.

Matt suddenly had a strange feeling that on the other side of that dark hedge he would find the dial on the tower, but large as the ring of the garden, a circle as wide as the children has made on the lawn, and perhaps its figures were alive too. Whether there were twelve or not, like the zodiac signs on the tower, signs of the months the sun passed through on his ever-returning journey, he did not know, but four he knew; the lion of the south, the human face to the west, the eagle in the north, and in the east the one he had not seen, the bull: four symbols of four ways of looking at the mystery that was both God and man.

He went through the gap in the hedge and there was the Rose Round; no roses on the bushes, only new leaves, and in the centre the broken fountain flinging up its fans of spray.

Matt went up to the middle and faced the eastern arch and shut his eyes, and saw again the cascades and festoons, the crown of roses there, the blush roses, whose hearts were golden pink and their outer petals pale as cream.

He opened his eyes and was almost dazzled. The sun's eye had lifted on the horizon and was shining directly into his own, under the brow of the eastern arch, and all the cloudy sky round it glowed like the hearts of roses, roses on fire.

The brightness of the sun's rising was a shock so keen that it sent a shiver of joy through Matt's body and he turned quickly round and looked to the centre. The fountain glittered and flashed in the new light like a rain of fire, and there, there was the bull's head for an instant clear and distinct in his eye, a great massive curly horned head faced to the orient sun.

To the east it looked, to the mountains of the beginning, to the caves of mystery, to the place where life rises out of darkness, the garden of creation and the tomb of resurrection.

Then it was gone and Matt knew he had seen it with his inward and not his outward eye, and that it was not less real for that. Signs of mystery, Theo had said, when he had seen the eagle in the north, before the hard winter and the time he had fallen off the roof. Theo wore an eagle in his ring, on his hand; it was his sign as well as St John's, the great bird king of the air who flew unblinded towards the sun. But this bull-head was not less his, nor the lion and the man looking west, and Matt felt that they were his own too, and any man's, and in every man they lived.

But bulls are dangerous and wild, Matt thought, and lions too: they were beasts of the forest and the great plains and of desert and mountain, and were they hiding inside people, inside himself? Suppose the bull charged? The lion roared upon its prey? The eagle swooped on its victim? Suppose the man should change his face and become any or all of these, and no longer human? He was suddenly afraid; it was not only dangerous, it was terrifying to be alive, to be someone with all these unknown powers in his heart.

Then he saw Theo come through the western arch on the other side of the fountain, looking at the sun rising, and at him too.

'Theo,' he said, holding on to the stone basin with his hands and looking through the falling water. 'I was thinking about the bull, and the others, how dangerous they are. Suppose they got loose? I know they're not real animals, but they are sort of real inside, aren't they? Suppose they did?'

'Well, they do sometimes,' said Theo, smiling. He came up to the fountain. 'They get very wild. Why do you think our world is in such confusion, with nations all quarrelling and fighting, and people grabbing everything they can from each other, and making silly excuses to justify themselves? The beasts inside have got loose.'

'I don't like them then,' said Matt. Yet he had, in fact, felt only wonder and delight when he had seen them, and a kind of awe.

'Yes, you do like them,' said Theo. 'They are splendid. They are all kings. They are what makes you a king too. You are a man in your mind, an eagle in your spirit, a lion in the courage of your will.'

'But the bull?'

'He's in the power of love,' said Theo.

Matt said, 'But they do go wild, you said so.'

'Yes, they go wild,' said Theo. 'But look at the garden: it's a square, but a square in a circle. It has a centre. Don't you remember talking about it on the tower?'

'The sun,' said Matt. 'The sun is the centre.'

'The sun is the centre outside,' said Theo. 'It is the image of the one who is inside: *Lux umbra Dei*.'

Matt looked at the golden sun rising. 'If he's in the centre, all's well with the sacred beasts,' said Theo. 'The Phoenix is their Lord.'

The sun was shining in his nest of clouds, brighter and brighter, like the Phoenix in the rose of fire. Matt looked back at the fountain, the water that sprang up and fell back for ever.

'Then why is it Our Lady who is here in the middle the garden, Theo? Why not him?'

'Because this is our world,' said Theo. 'He chose to come into it through her. He is too great to fit into the ring of the world, this little pattern of our sun and our hearts, except by becoming her child, and so one of us. And yet if you look at it inside out you will see that all this, the solar circle, the seasons of time, the fountain of life, the fourfold living signs of the soul, and the Lady herself who said yes to the will of love, are all in him, only in him, and we see them clearer when we look at them in him. There are some people who will only see everything in themselves, but don't be one of them. Our selves are only moons in his sun: in his light all things are revealed as they are.'

Now the sun had risen above the arch and shone down on them, sweeping the whole earth with the beams of its brilliance.

They heard Caro calling in the garden.

'Matt, where are you?'

'He's here with me,' Theo answered her. 'In the Rose Round.'